Author's Note

This story was originally published as 'The Drums of Anfield' in the summer of 2000. It attracted widespread acclaim for the way it addressed issues of racism and prejudice.

'The Drums of Hampden' was made possible by the support of Sense over Sectarianism. Sense over Sectarianism is a partnership with funding from the Millennium Commission to give grants to people setting up projects or programmes that challenge sectarianism and bigotry in the wider Glasgow area.

The partners in the project are:

Glasgow City Council
Nil By Mouth
Celtic FC
Rangers FC
The Glasgow Presbytery of the Church of Scotland
The Roman Catholic Archdiocese

Acknowledgements

To Carol who is always there to tell me that I can do this.

To my boys who were my first audience.

To Yasmin for putting up with ridiculous deadlines

and to Alison for managing to keep the cogs turning!

Thanks to the pupils of Loreburne School in Dumfries

for helping me with the cover design.

The Drums
of Hampden

Mark Frankland

A Glenmill Publication

First published in 2002

Glenmill

Dumfries

Scotland

DG2 8PX

tel: 0776 149 3542

http://www.thecull.com

British Library Cataloguing in Publication Data.
A catalogue record of this book is available from the British Library.

Printed and bound in Great Britain by Cox & Wyman Ltd, Reading

ISBN 0 9535944 6 7

Contents

Chapter 1
Old Enemies

September
European Championship Group Stage Qualifier
England v Scotland

The ball was clipped through from the right back. Tony reacted instantly. He flew across the pitch and slid toward the ball. It was gone. Jimmy Stamp took it right off Tony's boot and sprinted towards the goal. A deafening "Ooooooh" poured down from the packed stands as Stamp blasted his shot inches over the bar.

The near-miss switched the noise of the crowd up to a new ear-splitting level. Tony heaved himself off the ground and stood bent over with his hands on his knees. He tried to drag air into his lungs and his heart was pounding painfully. He glanced up at the scoreboard and saw to his relief that there were only seconds to go before half-time.

His left leg was burning with pain. He mentally cursed himself for insisting on playing, even though his injury wasn't properly healed.

He felt a hand ruffle his hair and turned around sharply. It was Stamp. Jimmy Stamp, the 21-year-old Londoner who was the new pin-up boy of the English Premier League.

"Bit tired are we Hobbo? Well it's a hard game for an old man."

Tony snarled, but before he had chance to say anything Stamp was gone. He caught the signal from the keeper and drifted into the centre circle. The ball was rolled to Davie

1

Tarrant. As tarrant held the ball, Tony made a fast break to the edge of the centre circle. Tarrant clipped the ball forward toward him. It was perfect. Tony saw from the corner of his eye that Bobby Simms, his centre forward, was making his break exactly on cue.

It was a move that they had practised hard in training. All Tony needed to do now was to flick a curled ball down the left wing and Simms was clear. He moved easily to the ball, but his leg let him down. As he was about to make the pass a red-hot pain lanced up his leg and he miss hit his pass horribly.

Instead of curling down the wing the ball flew into the crowd. A wave of mockery and laughter poured down from the stands.

The referee blew his whistle. Half-time. At last.

As Tony made his way off the pitch he concentrated hard on not limping. The crowd was taunting him and he tried to blot the noise out.

As Stamp trotted past him he shouted "Nice ball old man." and laughed. Tony gritted his teeth and doggedly made his way toward the tunnel.

Once inside the dressing room he flopped down onto the bench and hung a towel over his head. He allowed the wave of tiredness to wash over him.

Tony Hobbes was 33 and he had been playing for Scotland since the age of 19. For the last three seasons he had been the captain. He was a central midfielder. He had never been known as a flair player, he was a hard tackling ball winner. He had been issued his fair share of yellow cards in his time.

He had broken into senior football for Queens Park when he was seventeen. Two years later he had moved to Partick Thistle and was soon spotted as a player of the future. Pundits spoke of him growing into the next great Scottish hard man midfielder in the mould of Billy Bremner and Graham Souness. Three weeks before his 21st birthday he was signed by Liverpool for £250,000 and he soon became a first team regular.

His 100 percent effort and his crunching tackling had always made him a great favourite of the Liverpool crowd. Whenever he clattered an opponent the supporters would always gleefully chant "Hobbo! Hobbo!"

He had graced the hallowed Anfield turf for eleven glorious years until at last age began to get the better of him. Younger men were coming into the frame and he saw that his days in the first team were numbered. The club had no hesitation in recognising his magnificent service by granting him a free transfer. He had lots of options and lots of offers, however there was only one which really appealed to him. He went back to his roots. He went back to Partick Thistle as club captain.

The frantic speed and passion of Scottish football gave him a new lease of life. Tony's presence galvanised Partick and under his driving captaincy they had won promotion back to the SPL.

However this season he was finding that every game was getting harder. His pace had deserted him and he had to rely more and more on his experience and instinct. To compensate for his loss of speed he had started to play in a deeper and more defensive role. A strong tackle in an away trip to Hibernian had left him with a badly bruised Achilles heel. He had missed four games and felt that he needed at least another three games off, before the injury was properly healed. Normally he would have taken the rest and done the right thing. But not this time. No way.

When the draw had been made for the qualifying group for the 2004 European Championships the football world had buzzed with excitement. Italy, England, Scotland, Latvia and Luxembourg. Amazing.

Scotland had beaten Luxembourg home and away. They had edged a narrow win in Latvia and been held to a goalless draw at home to the Italians. England on the other hand had won every game and pulled out one of their finest efforts in years to defeat the mighty Italians 3 – 1 in Milan. Jimmy Stamp had scored twice and the English media had gone into overdrive. It seemed like every TV station had showed the England goals at least twenty times a day.

There was a month's gap until football's oldest of enemies were due to clash at Old Trafford in the second qualifying match. As each day passed the papers gave Scotland less and less chance. The new young England side was one of the best anyone had seen in years. Jimmy Stamp had the ability to become one of the greatest players in the world. Scotland on the other hand was lagging far behind. They had no star players and they had been slowly sliding down hill for years. What chance had they against the new sparkling youngsters who had taken the Italians by storm? None. None whatsoever.

Tony had felt a boiling anger growing inside him as he suffered the endless media build up. With a week to go to the game nobody gave Scotland a chance. Bill Duncan, the Scotland Manager had called him on the Monday night.

"How's the leg Hobbo?"

"Fine boss. No problems."

"Are you sure?"

He had laughed. "The only way I wouldn't be sure is if someone came and cut it off boss. Light training and a pain killing jab. That's all I need. There's no way I'm missing this one. No way at all."

In fact he had barely trained at all. The leg was hurting almost all the time but he was determined not to show it. He knew that the manager was worried. Of course he was. Tony would have to try and stop Jimmy Stamp and anchor the midfield. If he wasn't 100% . . . the manager said that had to be sure. He just had to be sure. And Tony kept on telling him that he was fine. No problem. Just wait and see.

Even if his leg had been perfect he would have found it tough to keep up with Stamp. The boy was twelve years younger and twice as quick. It had only been Tony's vast experience that had enabled to keep the Londoner in check. But as the first 45 minutes wore-on he could feel the leg becoming more and more painful.

As he sat under his towel he had to admit to himself that Stamp had so far had the best of the battle. However all was not lost. By a mixture of luck and desperate defending Scotland had managed to keep a clean sheet, and as long as the score was 0 – 0 there was always hope.

Duncan was frantically trying to build his players up for the second half. Tony closed his eyes and did his best to block out the sound. Could he make it? Was he really being fair to his team-mates? Maybe he should call it a day. The manager came and sat down next to him.

"I have to ask you straight Hobbo. Can you make it? We need you out there. The younger players are only just managing to hold it together. We need an old head. Another 45 minutes. That's all. Can you do it?"

Tony sat quietly for a moment and then slowly nodded. Duncan was right. It was only 45 minutes. Surely the leg would hold-out that long. He knew that what he was doing was stupid and that he was risking the rest of his career. He brushed the negative thoughts aside and waved over to Ken Timpson, the trainer.

"How is it Hobbo?"

"Lousy. I need another jab."

Timpson frowned. "Are you sure that's a good idea?"

Tony sighed. Of course it wasn't a good idea. It was an awful idea. He had met lots of retired players who were near cripples because they had played through their injuries by having too many pain killing injections.

"No it isn't a good idea but there isn't any choice. If I'm going to chase that little Cockney around the park for another 45 minutes I'm going to need something."

He winced as the needle was pushed into his leg and then allowed the numbness to spread. It was better. It was by no means good, but at least it was better. A bell rang outside in the corridor. He couldn't believe it. The fifteen minutes of half-time seemed to have gone by in a flash. Reluctantly he heaved himself to his feet and clapped his hands.

"OK boys, heads up. We stopped them first half. We can stop them again. Just keep concentrating and ignore the crowd. Let's do it."

As he ran out onto the pitch he felt a little better. The

effects of the injection were doing him a power of good. Again he clapped his hands and urged the players on.

For twenty minutes things went well. Scotland at last managed to get hold of the ball and they began to enjoy some decent periods of possession. England started to show signs of frustration. They started to hoof long balls forward, which the Scotland defence dealt with easily. Suddenly things were looking a lot more hopeful.

The England supporters were getting quieter and quieter as they became agitated and anxious. Suddenly it was the sound of the 8000 travelling Scots that dominated the stadium.

Scotland was steadily building up an attack down the left when Jimmy Stamp intercepted a pass and darted forward. Tony threw himself into the challenge but realised that he was too late a split-second before he crashed into Stamp's legs. The stadium erupted into a barrage of angry sound. Tony got up and waited nervously for the referee. The seconds ticked by with agonising slowness as the crowd bayed "OFF! OFF! OFF!". The ref reached into his pocket and pulled out a card. A wave of relief poured through Tony when he saw that the card was yellow. The crowd booed out their anger.

"Careful Hobbo." Said the referee. "One more like that and you're off."

The booking took away Scotland's rhythm and the English started to pour on the pressure again. In the 72nd minute, a slick move resulted in Stamp sprinting towards the goal. Tony moved in but realised at the last moment that once again he was too late. He just managed to pull out of the challenge that would have seen him sent off. The young Londoner swept past him and buried the ball into the far corner of the net.

The stadium erupted. Tony looked around his players and saw that their heads were down. He tried to encourage them but they already looked a beaten side. For a further ten minutes England piled on wave after wave of attacks and it was getting harder and harder to keep them out.

Again Stamp burst through, but this time he kicked the ball slightly too far ahead of himself. Tony lunged at the ball. To his horror and amazement the Englishman seemed to gain a miraculous turn of speed to clip the ball away from him.

Everything then went into a horrible slow motion. Tony was fully committed to the tackle and he could do nothing to stop it. He scythed through Stamp's legs and the Englishman went down as if a tank had shot him.

"OFF! OFF! OFF . . !"

As Tony tried to get up he felt a terrible pain shoot up through his leg. The tackle had done something dreadful to his injury. He had never known an injury to hurt as much. The ref was making his way across and reaching into his pocket. This time there was no doubt about what colour the card would be. The crowd was jubilant. The pain and the tension and tiredness made Tony feel almost dizzy.

And then Stamp was there. Up close. Pushing his face close to Tony's. "Is that all you're good for old man? Is that all you can do you codger? You're nothing but a carthorse, a useless nigger carthorse . . . "

Something snapped. The pain, the crowd, the mocking Cockney voice, the referee pulling out a red card, the racist jibe . . . all of a sudden it was too much. Tony was not aware of making any decision. He just did it. He hit Stamp hard on the nose and felt the bone crack.

He never looked back. He completely ignored the pain in his leg and jogged in a straight line to the tunnel.

*... Tony's father thundered his way up the
stairs. The bedroom door flew open and
Winston Hobbes stormed into the room.*

Chapter 2
Trouble

Somebody was shaking his shoulder. Tony came awake in a towering bad mood. Was there no peace to be had anywhere? His mood eased as he opened his eyes to see the face of his son, Ben.

"Oh Ben, do you have to? Just leave me for a little bit can you? What's the time anyway?"

"Ten past eight."

"Well give me until nine will you?"

Ben assumed an unhappy expression. "I can't"

"Why?"

"Cos Grandad's here. I came to warn you."

Tony groaned and sank back into the pillows. He winked at his son and said. "Try and fend him off for a bit will you Ben."

"Course I will dad, but . . . "

They both heard the heavy footsteps as Tony's father thundered his way up the stairs. The bedroom door flew open and Winston Hobbes stormed into the room.

"Benjamin, you go out now. You go out and wait downstairs with them women. Me and your daddy need to do some talkin'."

Ben gave his dad a sheepish glance then made his way out of the room and quietly closed the door behind him. Tony sat up painfully and eyed his father. There was little doubt that Winston Hobbes cast an impressive figure. He was six foot six inches tall and built like a battleship. As was the case every Sunday, he was wearing his best three-piece suit, a starched white shirt and a severe tie. As ever, it did not matter to Winston that his son was a mere six feet away

–he shouted as if he were somewhere in Govan on the other side of the Clyde.

"What is goin' on here boy? Why are you skulkin' and sulkin' in your bed. Get up man. No good hidin' yourself away. Get up and face things like a man. I'm not havin' no son of mine hidin' away in his bed like some two-bit cringin' coward just because . . . "

Tony held up his hands to try and stem the tide.

"Easy dad, it's only eight o'clock and it IS Sunday you know."

"Course I know that boy. I know that because I should be goin' to church to pray to the Lord, not havin' to come round here to sort out business."

Tony's face became suspicious. "What business Dad?"

"Your business boy. What else? Now you might think that you can hide away and pretend that nothin' has gone on, but not me. I am your father and I am your agent too. I have talked to Mr Duncan and I have talked to the people at the S.F.A. as well. We are seeing them both down at Hampden at 10.30 and we are goin' to sort things out."

"Oh Dad, did you have to . . . "

"Course I had to boy. Now get up out of that bed and get yourself ready. And take care to dress up smart because there are reporters waitin' in the road. Now move it."

Winston turned military style and walked out. Tony wondered for the thousandth time how it was that he was still being bossed about by his dad at the age of 33. How many other men had to put up with a dad like his? Not many. There again, how many men had a dad like his? Not many.

Tony had never met anyone quite like his father. He had got off the boat from Barbados in 1958 and had never left Glasgow. He had found work in the shipyards and had been there ever since. The other Glaswegian shipyard workers had soon learned that it was a bad idea to take the Mickey out of the giant West Indian. Over the years many had found out the hard way that it was a very bad idea to get on the wrong side of Winston Hobbes.

TROUBLE

It was not just his colour that set him apart from most of his workmates. He also didn't drink or smoke and never missed church on a Sunday. However he gradually became a figure of great respect. As the years passed he became one of the most senior figures in the Union.

When Tony had signed for Partick Thistle, his father had informed the club that he would act as his son's agent. Initially Tony had grave misgivings about the arrangement but he hadn't dared mention them to his father. These worries soon passed. Years of bargaining on behalf of the Union had made Winston Hobbes a very hard man to do business with. His powerful presence ensured that Tony always seemed to get a better contract than many of his fellow players. There were very few men around who would get the better of his father.

As he heaved himself out of bed and hobbled to the shower he grudgingly admitted to himself that his father was right. It was far better to go straight out and face the music rather than hiding away and waiting for the trouble to come to him.

As he allowed the hot water to wake him up he shuddered at the thought of how much trouble there was going to be. As he had sat in the dressing room the afternoon before he had heard the Old Trafford crowd roar a further three times in the last ten minutes. Without Tony to shore them up, the Scottish defence had caved in and England had gone on to win 4 – 0. It had been a humiliation. One of the worst defeats of a Scottish side in living memory.

Things had gone from bad to worse. A quick examination of his leg had shown that he had ripped a ligament and would be out of action for at least four months. The other players had barely said a word to him as they trudged into the dressing room. To make things worse, he had been pelted with fruit and coins as he had hobbled out of the ground and onto the team coach.

Later that night he had sat with his wife Karen and watched *Match of the Day*. It had been a miserable experience. Each of his late tackles on Stamp was shown over and over again in slow motion. They showed his punch six times. The England manager had been livid and demanded a severe punishment. Duncan had promised the cameras that the S.F.A. would be conducting a full enquiry and that disciplinary measures would be taken. Jimmy Stamp had given an interview from behind a plaster-cast on his broken nose. Both of his eyes had blackened and he had looked an awful mess. The panel in the studio all agreed that what Tony Hobbes had done was a disgrace to the game and that he should be severely punished. The S.F.A. had promised an enquiry.

Karen hadn't bothered to leave the tele on. She clicked it off with the remote control and folded her arms.

"Well Tony, I don't think that you are the most popular footballer in the world today."

"No."

"And I don't suppose they will be wanting you to do any *Coca Cola* adverts for a little while."

"No."

"But at least the worst is over."

Tony groaned. "No it isn't. The worst is still to come."

Karen smiled sadly. "Oh yes. Sorry. I forgot. Your Dad."

"Yes. My Dad. He's going to kill me."

As Tony hopped into the kitchen the silence was deafening. Winston was sitting bolt upright on a stool gazing fiercely into space. Ben was sitting at the table picking at his cereal. Karen and his mum were in the kitchen making coffee.

At the sight of her hopping son, his mother said in her native Glasgow accent. "Are you all right Tony? What have you done?"

He smiled at his mother. "Ligaments mum. I've torn them. I won't be playing for a while."

"More than he deserves." Growled Winston. "He deserves to have his leg cut off."

Ben's eyes widened in alarm. Winston noticed and ruffled his hair. "I'm only jokin' boy. Only jokin'. Now you get on and eat that breakfast all up now. When you've finished go and find that walkin' stick that your Daddy used when he broke his ankle. He can't go hoppin' around like some jumpy cat in front of all those newspaper reporters, now can he?"

The big man could not help but smile as he looked down into Ben's worried face. "Don't you worry boy, me and your Daddy are goin' to sort everythin' out."

Tony climbed onto the stool next to his father with difficulty and took a sip of coffee. He glanced at the back page of the paper then pushed it away. Predictably it was dominated by a huge photo of him landing his punch on Stamp's nose.

Winston glanced down at the photo. "Tell me Tony. Why did you do this thing? You've never done a thing like this before."

"I don't know Dad. Everything just got to me. I was an idiot for playing in the first place. There was no way that I was ready. I had to have to pain killing jabs just to get on the pitch at all, and you know how I hate to take them. I chased Stamp all over the park but I could never seem to catch him and he just kept on giving me lip. Then there was the crowd, and the red card, and he went and called me a "useless nigger" and something just snapped. I lost it. Simple as that."

Winston sat silent and still. Karen moved over to take Ben out of the room. Winston stopped her with a wave of his hand.

"Please Karen. I hope you don't mind, but Ben should stay and listen to these things. I know he is only seven years old but he is a little brown boy and he must learn."

Karen looked over to Tony who nodded.

"You listen well Benjamin. These are important things. When I came to Scotland many people called me a nigger. I would like to say that I did as the good Lord teaches and turned the other cheek. But I cannot say this. There were times when I did not do this. There were times that I did the same as your Daddy did and I knocked men to the ground. But I learned that it was wrong. Just because we are black we don't have the right to hit people for what they say. Now Benjamin, when some little boy calls you a nigger in the playground, and one day they will, you must not do the same thing as your Daddy. Is that right Tony?"

Tony nodded. "It's right Ben. What I did was wrong. He shouldn't have said what he said, but it was no excuse. I am ashamed of what I did. Never think it is right. Understood?"

Ben nodded. Tony took another sip of coffee. "I'm not going to mention the racism at any enquiry. It will only open a can of worms. I'll just say that he said some things and that I lost my rag. That's it. I'm not going to use it as an excuse."

Winston grinned and walloped his son on the back causing him to spit his mouthful of coffee onto the table.

"Good. That is what I was hopin' you would say. Now get your coat on and we will go."

When they got to the front door Winston said "You don't say anything to these paper men. Leave them to me."

As they walked down the path to the car the group of reporters swarmed toward them only to be stopped dead in their tracks by the roar of Winston's voice. "Get back now! Can't you see this is a badly injured man! Back!"

The gaggle of reporters duly obliged. "Now listen. We are on our way to a meeting with the S.F.A. We will make a statement after the meeting. That's it. You've all wasted your time. Now go home. Go to church. Go."

Before any of the reporters had the chance to speak the two men jumped into the car and drove away. Tony switched on the radio and scanned until he found a local talk show.

"OK, on the line we have Stan from Bellshill, morning Stan."

"Morning."

"And what would you like to say Stan?"

"I think Hobbo done right. You see what Stamp said. He called him a nigger didn't he. I reckoned he deserved to get planted."

"We have Ollie from Paisley. What do you say Ollie?"

"I say the same. I mean, I know you can't just go round belting people and that, but I reckon Stamp had it coming. I can't stand him, he's a right arrogant little . . . sorry, I can't think of what to say without swearing. But I'm with Hobbo. Us fans will stick with him, I just hope the S.F.A. does the same."

As they made their way into the city centre Tony was encouraged by the fact that almost all of the calls were supportive. It would be different elsewhere of course, especially in England, but at least it looked like his own fans were sticking by him.

When they were a mile from Hampden Winston switched off the radio. "Looks like you are going to get lucky boy. Everybody seems to know what he said. If you say nothin' about it you'll come out OK."

"How come?"

Winston grinned happily. "You just leave this to me boy."

A few minutes later they walked into the Chief Executive's sumptuous office overlooking the pitch. Sir Robert Hyde glanced up from the papers that he was working on and gave a brief smile. "Morning Tony, Morning Winston. Have a seat. I'll be with you in a minute."

They sat down and Sir Robert completed reading his document and signed it. He placed in his out-tray and looked up.

Bill Duncan who was sitting at the side of the desk spoke. "Morning Hobbo, not a very good time I'm afraid" He glanced over to Winston. "Who's this?"

"My Dad. He is my agent."

Sir Robert spoke in a businesslike tone. "Gentlemen, I am afraid that we are all facing a rather difficult situation. There is no point whatsoever in beating about the bush. Yesterday was one of the worst days for Scottish football that I can remember. In fact it is hard to imagine how it could have been any worse. Getting beaten 4 – 0 by England is bad enough. But your situation Tony, well, your situation is altogether more serious. You'll be aware that there has been a widespread clamour for the S.F.A. to take action. Drastic action."

Tony nodded.

"Good. Before we get into the nitty-gritty I would like to confirm one thing. Is it or is it not the case that Stamp made a directly racist comment that lead to you hitting-out."

Tony cleared his throat. "Within these four walls Sir Robert, the answer is 'yes', but it is not something that I want to make an issue out of. It's no excuse."

Sir Robert eyed Tony quizzically. "Are you entirely sure that is a wise course of action?"

Tony was about to reply when Winston raised his hand to silence him. "If you have no objections Sir Robert, I would like to make one or two suggestions."

The Chief executive sat back in his seat and nodded. Winston arranged some papers and then spoke. "There are several issues that need to be addressed here. As Tony has said, it is not our intention to use the racist issue as any kind of excuse. What he did was completely inexcusable. It is quite understandable that there is such a widespread demand for action.

"I have studied the details of the contract that all players abide by when they play for the National side. Unlike in club football, the National side has little ability to punish its players financially for any misdemeanours. As we all know, the match fee for representing Scotland is a mere £300 – chicken feed. Were the S.F.A. merely to withold this sum of money then it would be seen as not being nearly enough. We would agree with that judgement"

This made Tony's eyes widen but he kept quiet.

"This means that the only real punishment available to the S.F.A. and Mr Duncan is to ban Tony from playing for Scotland for a very long time. I can assure you that this is the outcome that we wish to avoid at all costs. In the light of this, we propose that Tony presents Mr Finnighan with a cheque for £10,000 to donate to a charity of his choice as evidence of our absolute remorse for what has happened. We have tickets for the two o'clock flight to London and it is our intention to make the presentation at Mr Stamp's home with the press present. Tony will apologise in person."

It was hard to tell who was the most astonished at Winston's suggestion – Tony or Bill Duncan or Sir Robert. At last Sir Robert spoke "Well Mr Hobbes. What can I say? I congratulate you for your wisdom. Such a press conference will do a power of good for our reputation. Consider your proposal agreed. The S.F.A. will fully support your magnificent gesture. I have only one concern Winston. England. Will they play ball? I don't think that they will like the idea of our coming out of this thing looking good."

Winston smiled a big broad smile. "Everybody knows exactly what Mr Stamp said to Tony. Now we will not make an issue of this unless they force us to. Now I think if you make a call to your opposite number in the English F.A. and tell him this, I am sure that he will be happy to co-operate. After all, they wouldn't want to see their prize asset accused of calling people niggers would they."

Sir Robert couldn't help it. He laughed. "Mr Hobbes, you're a genius. I'll ring him this morning. I'll look forward to it. Now is there anything else?"

Winston spoke. "There is the issue of the captaincy. We will of course offer to resign . . . "

Sir Robert picked up the sentence straight away . . . and we of course will not accept it."

Bill Duncan grinned.

"Good." Said Sir Robert. "Then that concludes our business for today. There will be more I'm afraid. You will of course receive a three match international ban for the sending off and the S.F.A. will certainly have to charge you with bringing the game into disrepute. However all is not as bad as it seems. I gather you have aggravated your injury somewhat Tony."

"I'm afraid so Sir Robert. I've torn my ligaments. I'll be out for at least four months."

The Chief Executive gave a sly grin. "Well the international ban will mean that you miss the three friendlies that we have lined up. Happily you will be available for selection for the home game against Latvia and the trip to Rome in the spring. The disrepute charge will mean a domestic ban of several games but it would appear that you would be injured for these anyway. I know that this is very much out of character for you Tony. Let's try and put it all behind us as best as we can shall we?"

"Definitely Sir Robert."

Sir Robert looked at his watch. "Well, I'm afraid that the next job is the press. It's a drag but it has to be done. I think that I will come and sit in on this one. I have told everyone to be in the Media Centre for 11 o'clock. We'd best go."

When tea was finished they all headed out onto the front steps of the house and the photographers took the pictures of Jimmy and Tony shaking hands which would dominate the back pages of the next day's papers.

Chapter 3
Public Relations

As they walked out the Chairman's office Winston said. "We have a few minutes to spare. Give me that mobile telephone."

"Who are you ringing?" Tony asked suspiciously.

"Wait and see."

Winston pulled a small notebook from his pocket, found a number and dialed. As the phone was answered he glanced up and down the corridor to make sure that nobody was listening.

"Good morning. Is that Mrs Stamp? This is Winston Hobbes speakin', I'm Tony's daddy. Listen Mrs Stamp, I'm feelin' real bad about what my boy gone and done to your boy. I'm afraid where I come from it is always left to us parents to sort out the mess that our kids leave behind. I guess that it is the same in London. It is? I thought so. Now listen, my boy and me have just had a big tellin' off from the Chief Executive of the S.F.A. He told Tony that they were goin' to fine him the whole of his match fee but Tony is feelin' so bad about what has happened that he is going to pay much, much more. £10,000 in fact. Now the Chief Executive has agreed that all of the money should be given to your boy to give to a charity.

"Now we've got to go and talk to the newspapers now, but when we're through we would like to fly down and see your boy. Tony wants to apologise in person. This thing wants calmin' down straight away. Your boy got a little excited and said some bad things about Tony's colour and Tony got even more excited and went and hit him. None of this does any good. We don't want to make an issue of the colour thing. Could you ring your boy and persuade him to see us?

Good. Thank you Mrs Stamp. I'll call you in five minutes to make sure it is OK."

Winston snapped the phone shut and grinned with delight. Tony rolled his eyes. "Why is it that I feel that my life isn't my own any more."

His father said in a stern voice. "Because you behaved like a fool and broke a man's nose."

Jimmy Stamp's mother duly informed Winston that she had persuaded her son to see them and they marched into the press conference in the John Logie Baird Suite. The room was packed. Sir Robert was already inside sitting with Bill Duncan. Winston and Tony joined them and Sir Robert stood up and addressed the waiting journalists.

"Good morning gentlemen. Thank you for coming at such short notice. I can inform you that myself and Mr Duncan have had a meeting with Tony Hobbes and his father Winston Hobbes who acts as the player's agent. We have discussed the events of yesterday and have implemented a disciplinary procedure. I feel that it would be best if Winston Hobbes informs you of the details of this procedure, as they are somewhat unusual. I can also inform you that I have spoken to my opposite number at the English F.A. this morning and he has indicated his satisfaction with the measures that the S.F.A. has taken concerning this issue. To conclude I would like to emphasise how seriously we are viewing this issue and how profoundly sad we are that it has happened. However I must say that I have been delighted with response that our captain has made and I feel that it should be viewed very positively.

"Winston, maybe you could say a few words."

Winston stood up to his full height and surveyed the room. When he spoke his voice boomed and the journalists flinched. "What happened yesterday was a disgraceful thing and Tony fully accepts this. There are no excuses for what he did and he is going to offer a full apology to Mr Stamp. After this meeting Tony and me are goin' to fly to London and apologise to Jimmy in person. You are all welcome to come with us. The rules of the S.F.A. allow for Tony to be fined the whole of his match fee for what he did. This represents the princely sum of £300. Tony doesn't feel that this is enough. He is therefore going to present a cheque for £10,000 to Jimmy Stamp to donate to a charity of his choice.

"Very few men go right through life without makin' a mistake. Tony has just made a very big one. He knows this and he intends to pay for it. He is upset at what he did. He can't say any more. Thank you.'

Sir Robert asked for questions and a forest of hands was raised.

"A question for Tony. Tony, is it the case that Jimmy Stamp called you a nigger and that is why you hit him?"

Tony considered his answer carefully. "I have been a pro for sixteen years and things have always gone on on the pitch. The difference now is that there are so many cameras taking close up shots of the players. As far as I am concerned anything that is said on the field of play is a private matter. What I will say is that there is nothing that Jimmy could have said to me that would have justified what I did."

"But Tony, DID he say it?"

"I think that I have answered the question."

"Tony, don't you think that the fans have a right to know what was really said?"

Winston learned forward and spoke in a fierce voice. "Now you all listen. Jimmy Stamp is one of the finest players in the game today. He had a brilliant game yesterday. Today he is in pain with a broken nose. No player deserves that. Now please will you accept that anything that he said to Tony was a private matter? Tony did wrong and he is makin' no excuses. That is the end of the matter."

It wasn't of course. The reporters made desperate efforts to get a response on the racist issue but got absolutely nowhere. The meeting was eventually brought to a close and the reporters filed out feeling that they had been cheated. When the room was finally empty Tony sank back into his chair and whistled.

Sir Robert patted him on the shoulder. "Good effort Tony. I think that things will blow over now. Just get your head down and concentrate of getting fit for the spring."

Tony and Winston caught their plane and were met by a several journalists at the other end. Accompanied by the gaggle of reporters, they headed out of London to Jimmy Stamp's house. Jimmy's mother welcomed Winston like a long lost relative and they chatted on happily over tea. Tony and Jimmy were not as comfortable. They sipped their tea in silence until Tony felt that he had to say something.

"Look Jimmy I was out of order. I'm sorry OK. How's the nose?"

"Hurts like hell." Jimmy's voice came out slurred.

"Well let's bury the hatchet shall we?"

"We'll see."

Tony couldn't think of anything more to say. He didn't seem to be getting very far. In fact it was Stamp who spoke. "I murdered you yesterday Hobbo. You're too slow. Your legs have gone."

"I was injured. Next time I'll be fit. Then we'll see."

"Yeah, we will."

After that they fell back into silence. When tea was finished they all headed out onto the front steps of the house and the photographers took the pictures of Jimmy and Tony shaking hands which would dominate the back pages of the next day's papers.

As they headed back towards the airport Tony said. "Well I sure am glad that that's all over." He looked over to his father who was giving his full attention to the road. "Thanks Dad."

Winston grinned. "I was wonderin' when you would get round to sayin' that. Think nothin' of it, this is why you have an agent. You just do one thing for me."

"What's that."

"You go and get yourself fitter than you ever been before, and next time you come up against that skinny, big-mouthed Londoner . . . you take him to the cleaners."

"It will be a pleasure."

Chapter 4
Africa

After all the excitement of the September weekend, life soon started to drag for Tony. It came as little surprise to him when he was told that his leg needed an operation. This was carried out the next week and meant that he had to suffer hobbling around in plaster for a month and a half.

He was called in for the S.F.A. Disciplinary committee at the end of the month. It was a painful experience. He received a nine-match ban. The worst thing was that he had become branded as a complete nutter.

This new reputation did him little harm in Glasgow. The fans by and large were delighted that he had thumped Jimmy Stamp and he was fast becoming something of a cult figure. It had been a great relief to discover that his action had not caused Ben any problems at school. In fact the opposite had occurred. Having the Scotland captain as his dad had always given Ben extra kudos with his classmates. Having the Scotland captain who had broken Jimmy Stamp's nose seemed to give him even more.

Tony decided to make the most of his enforced idleness and spend as much time as possible with his family. He had been married to Karen for thirteen years. She was a nurse at one of the big hospitals in the city. He had met her when he had stayed overnight at the Victoria Infirmary near Hampden Park having received concussion during a Partick home match against Motherwell.

As Tony's career had taken off Karen had shown no wish to give up her own career. Over the years she had studied hard and ground her way through a series of stiff exams. She was in line to become a Ward Sister within the next couple of years. It all made Tony feel rather guilty. He worked for three hours a day and played football on a Saturday and Tuesday night. Karen worked at least ten hours a day and often weekends as well. He felt guilty because at the peak of his career with Liverpool he was earning more in a fortnight than she earned in a year and he didn't even work a quarter as hard. To try and make up for this he had made the decision early on to do all he could to help out with raising Ben. He had always taken him to school in the morning and collected him in the afternoon.

During school holidays he had always taken Ben with him to training where the ground staff were more than happy to keep him amused whilst the team were put through their paces.

Tony had been nervous when he took Ben to school the Monday morning after the Old Trafford game. He was worried about how the other parents would react. There was no need. A number of fathers came over to shake his hand

and several mothers told him of what a wonderful gesture it had been to donate his fine to charity.

He found the same reception whenever he was out in the city. It soon became clear that nobody in Scotland had much love for Jimmy Stamp. His only real problem had come when the headmaster had called him in to inform him that Ben had been fighting. The poor man tiptoed around the issue and was obviously scared that Tony was about to thump him.

This saddened Tony. He was not a violent man and never had been. What he had done had been totally out of character but he knew that it would live with him for a long time. Some enterprising firm had printed up T-shirts with Jimmy Stamp's battered face on the front and Tony decked out like Mel Gibson in *Braveheart* on the back. These soon became all the rage across the country.

The plaster finally came off at the end of October and Tony was able to start very light exercise. He spent a lot of time walking and cycling and made sure that he spent at least two hours a day in the gym. Each day his leg felt a little better but he had been told not to even think of kicking a football until at least December.

It was ridiculous, but he was becoming super-fit in all the areas that didn't really matter for football. He was lifting heavier and heavier weights in the gym and he could cycle flat-out for well over half an hour.

By the beginning of December the frustration was beginning to get him down. He spent a couple of hours with Ken Timpson who watched him complete a few exercises and X-rayed his leg.

"Look Tony, things are going fine but you mustn't push it too hard. There is no way that I will let you start playing until at least February. I know that you are feeling loads better but these things take time. I have seen far too many players try to come back too soon and it can do a heap of damage. Maybe it would be different if you were 23 Tony, but you're not. You're 33, and the older you get the longer it takes. You will only get one shot at this Tony. If you allow your leg to heal properly and take your time, you can play on for at least another three years. If you push it and come back too soon, it could be curtains."

Tony walked around the room impatiently. He couldn't believe it. Another two and a half months! He would go stark staring mad. "OK Ken, I can see where you are coming from. So what do I do? Just keep bashing away in the gym and on the bike?"

Timpson considered this. "No. Believe it or not, that is probably the worst thing that you can do. If you keep pushing yourself this hard you are going to do more harm than good. I think that the best thing is if you cut right down now. Just do some very light exercise and give your body time. Eat well. Take lots of vitamins and be patient. Don't flog yourself, it will only make the recovery time longer."

Tony couldn't believe it. "So what am I going to do Ken? It's only the training that is keeping me sane. I swear, if I have to open another supermarket I'll go mad."

"Go away Tony. Take a break. School holidays are coming soon. Take the family away somewhere. Make sure that it is somewhere nice and warm. Rest and warmth. I promise you that will be the best thing."

Tony considered this. It had been ages since he had the time to take the family on a proper holiday. The demands of the long football season coupled with the demands of Karen's work made it almost impossible. He smiled. "Ken, I owe you one. That is a really good idea.

Tony raised the matter of the holiday later that evening when he and Karen were sitting in the lounge as Ben was watching the *National Geographic* Channel.

"What do you think love?"

Karen pondered the question. "I think that it is a marvellous idea, just what you need. I'm afraid that I am the problem. I may be able to get away for a week but they wouldn't give me any longer. You know how things are at the hospital at Christmas, it is chaos."

Tony shrugged. "Well, a week it will have to be then."

"No." Said Karen. "No, that's silly. Why should I spoil things for the two of you. Why don't I come along for a week and the two of you stay on for another fortnight. I quite agree with Ken, warmth and rest will be the best thing for you Tony, and a week simply isn't enough."

Tony was appalled. "But we can't do that. That would mean that we would be away for Christmas and you would be all alone here."

She smiled. "Don't be silly Tony. I'm a big girl you know. To be honest it will be good for me to put the extra time in so that some of the younger ones can take time off. Honestly, I don't mind, and I will still have a week away. Where would you like to go? Back to Barbados again?"

"Well yes, I thought so. You know how dad feels about us keeping in touch with family. Does that suit you?"

"Of course it does. Barbados is always lovely at this time of year."

"OK then. Barbados it is."

Ben turned around from the television. "Dad."

"Yes."

"Could we go and see the animals instead?"

Tony was confused. "What animals?"

Ben pointed to the screen. It showed a herd of zebra grazing whilst two lions waited patiently in the long grass. "Those animals. The ones in Africa. Lions and elephants and hippos. Can we Dad?"

Tony looked across to Karen in astonishment. Africa! He had never even dreamed of going to Africa. And yet as soon as Ben spoke the word something stirred in him. Africa. It had a kind of magic sound. He remembered his father talking to him as a boy about Africa and it occurred that a small part of himself was African. One day long, long ago a distant relative must have been rounded up by slavers and taken to be sold in the West Indies. And of course a small part of Ben was African too.

The more he thought the more the idea thrilled him. Ben had always adored animals and he always preferred the animal documentaries to the cartoons. To see the animals in the wild would be fantastic. He looked over to Karen wondering what she would say. "Well love, what do you think?"

27

She laughed. "One look at your face tells me all that I need to know about what you think. I think that it is a fabulous idea. One of the nurses went to Kenya last summer. They had a sort of split holiday. They spent half the time on the beach and half the time on safari. We could do the same. I will come with you for a week on the beach and you two can go off for a fortnight's safari on your own. Now that would be smashing."

"And you really don't mind us being away for Christmas."

"Not at all. Make the most of this injury, you may never have time like this again, and Ben will certainly never be seven again. Let's do it."

Tony turned to his son. "Well partner, it looks like we are on. It will be me and you and the African bush."

Ben leapt to his feet and yelled with excitement.

Two weeks later after a long, hard flight they checked into their hotel on the beach at Malindi on the coast of the Indian Ocean. It was a beautiful hotel and the white sandy beaches seemed to go on forever. In others ways it reminded Tony a lot of Barbados but in many ways it was very different. He was disturbed when the hotel manager told them that it was very dangerous to walk far along the beach as tourists were often beaten-up and robbed. When he went into the small town he was shocked by the poverty. The houses on the outskirts of the town seemed to be made out of little more than cardboard.

They had a pretty good week but it was hardly peaceful. Most of the residents of the hotel were British, and many of them felt that it was fair enough for them to collar Tony and talk about football. Word soon spread among the waiters that he was Tony Hobbes, captain of Scotland, and every morning growing gangs of children waited outside to get his autograph. He resented this a great deal less than the drunken Brits who wouldn't leave the family alone in the restaurant. He had never had this kind of problem in Barbados as he could always go into his father's village to escape from the other tourists. He also realised that he had become a rather more famous person since he had laid-out Jimmy Stamp.

At the end of the week it was time for Karen to leave. They all took a flight up to Nairobi, the capital of Kenya. At the airport they had to wait for two hours until Karen got on the flight for London.

She gave them both a hug and wished them the best of luck in the bush. For a little while Ben was a bit quiet as their bus made its way out of the city and south. Tony himself felt rather flat as he watched the landscape outside the window. It wasn't at all what he had expected. Nairobi was 5,000 feet above sea level, which meant that the weather was cloudy and chilly and the landscape outside was flat and boring. There were no animals to be seen, just fields of crops and cattle and the occasional downbeat town.

However as they drove south they started to lose altitude and the landscape changed. Ben fell asleep for three hours and when he woke up everything was different. The country was drier and more like he had seen on the Tele. Eventually they passed a sign that informed them that they were entering the Amboseli game reserve and Ben became excited as he started to see more and more animals through the window of the bus.

They had booked onto a two-week safari that would take them around several of the best game parks in Kenya, starting with Amboseli. Each game park boasted a superb luxury lodge to stay in and special Land Rovers to take them out into the bush.

The first three days were wonderful. Amboseli was a truly beautiful place to be, especially in the early morning. They got up a little after five and joined the first safari of the day. It was the perfect time to be out. As the big sun climbed into the sky it coloured the snow on the top of the massive Mount Kilimanjaro amazing red and orange colours. Dawn was the time when the animals would come to the waterholes to drink, and in three days they saw nearly all the animals that Ben had longed for.

THE DRUMS OF HAMPDEN

By the end of each day Ben was tired out with all the excitement and fresh air and he would be fast asleep by seven o' clock.

After three days at Amboseli they got onto the bus and headed south for Tsavo. This was a different game park all together. It was absolutely massive and stretched for the same distance as Glasgow to London. It was much drier than Amboseli and more like a desert. Tony felt a tremendous surging feeling as they went for mile after mile down the dusty tracks of the park seeing absolutely nobody.

This he felt was the real Africa, a hard, beautiful empty place. It thrilled him. He felt rather differently about where they were staying, another beautiful lodge in the small village of Voi. It was luxuriously comfortable but somehow it didn't feel right. Every time they drove through another poor, dusty village Tony felt more and more awkward about staying in such luxury. He also felt that he was missing something. He was keen to see Africa but he was only seeing a very small part of it. At times he felt as if he was in a cinema, looking out from air-conditioned luxury. It bothered him greatly that he didn't seem to be meeting any Africans and he really wasn't learning anything about how they lived.

Once again the tourists were beginning to get on his nerves. He never seemed to get a moment's peace as they pestered him constantly. Their third day in Tsavo was a Saturday. They had been out all afternoon on a game run and Ben was tired out. Tony had taken him to his room for a nap and he had decided to have a wander about. He suddenly remembered the time difference. 5.30 in Kenya was 3.30 in Scotland. He chuckled as he realised that he had quite forgotten that the football season was still going on thousands of miles away. He thought for a moment and remembered that the Old Firm Match was being played that very minute.

There was already half an hour gone. How on earth could he find out the score? He saw one of the drivers working on the engine of his Land Rover at the edge of the car park. He was called Thomas and he had often talked to Tony about football as they had driven around. Tony walked across to where he was tinkering with the engine.

"Hi Thomas."

Thomas pulled himself out of the engine and beamed as he wiped his oily hands on a piece of rag. "Hello Mr Tony. How are you?"

"Oh fine, but I could do with a bit of help."

"If it is possible for me to be of an assistance Mr Tony, it would make me very happy."

"Do you have a radio?"

"Yes Mr Tony. A radio is something that I have."

"Great. Now listen Thomas. Celtic and Rangers are playing this afternoon and I would really like to listen to it on the World Service."

Thomas beamed even wider. "Of course you will want to hear this. I know that it is a very important game. I believe it is what you call the Old Firm Match."

"Bang right, Thomas. So could you come round to my room with the radio. I'd come with you but I can't leave Ben, he's asleep you see."

"But of course Mr Tony. I will be there in no longer time than ten minutes. But tell me just one thing. Why is it that they call this game the 'Old Firm Match'?"

Tony laughed. "To be honest Thomas, I have often wondered the same thing myself. I'm afraid that I haven't got a clue!"

Thomas was true to his word and turned up with his radio ten minutes later. They were in time for the second half. Tony pulled a couple of beers out of the mini-bar and they both sat listening happily as the little radio at times seemed like it would burst open with the sound of the crowd.

The game ended in a draw and Tony's feeling of contentment was somewhat disturbed by the news that Partick had crashed to a 4 – 0 defeat at Aberdeen. They had been slipping down the SPL steadily since his injury and now they were getting dangerously close to the relegation zone.

Thomas looked heavily serious. "It is indeed a very poor result Mr Tony. I feel that the team must be feeling your loss."

"Well thanks for your confidence Thomas, but . . . "

A man in a suit who had walked up to the veranda where they were sitting interrupted him. He was one of the under-managers from the hotel's reception area.

"Excuse me Mr Hobbes, but is this man bothering you?"

Tony was amazed. "No. Of course he isn't. He has kindly brought me a radio to listen to the football commentary. Why do you ask?"

"Sorry sir. Staff boys are not allowed to go to tourist's rooms. It is a rule of the hotel. It is best if he goes now."

"Best for who?" Tony was starting to get angry.

Thomas spoke quietly so that the manager could not hear him. "Please do not upset him Mr Tony. It will be bad for me." Then in a louder voice. "Thank you Mr Tony. I will go now."

He picked up his radio and left.

Ben woke up a few minutes later and Tony took him across the car park to where Thomas was once again working on his engine.

"I hope that you won't be in any trouble Thomas, I had no idea. If there is anything that I can do to help just say."

Thomas smiled. "No Mr Tony. Thank you, but there is no need. I have some difficulty with these people here."

Tony was confused. "Why?"

"Because I am not from here Mr Tony. My home is Uganda. There is no work for me in my own country so I have to come here. These boss men are all Kikuyu people. Kikuyu men not like Ugandans. It can be hard."

This saddened Tony. The only racism that he had ever known was white against black. It seemed almost worse when it was black against black. "I'm sorry to hear this Thomas. Maybe you could help me again. There is one thing that is disappointing me about my trip here. I never really seem to meet any African people. Where do you go on a Saturday night? Maybe you could take us with you? I'll square it with the manager first of course."

Once again Thomas grinned hugely. "This I can do Mr

Tony. I go to a small bar in the village of Voi. You will like it. They cook very good chicken and play good music. Many people go there. Kikuyu, Masai, Tanzanian, Ugandan, many. You will like it there."

"Then we're on. What time?"

"I will pick you up at 7.00 o' clock."

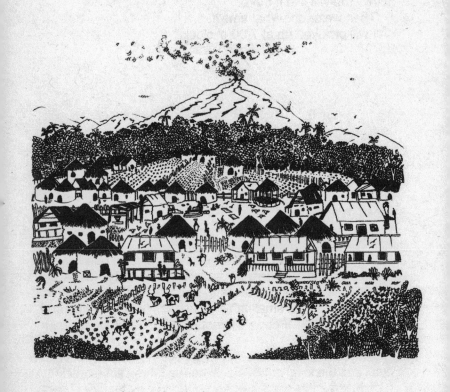

Chapter 5
Uganda

As soon as Tony and Ben walked into the restaurant with Thomas that evening he knew that he was going to like it. The name, which was hand-painted on to an old piece of timber by the door, made him smile. It was called "The Great Western Eating House." It was hard to see where the "Great" came from but it certainly reminded him of a Western. The big shack seemed to be entirely built from rusty pieces of corrugated iron and it was more-or-less held together with string.

What was certain was that it was popular. Loud African music beat hard and every table seemed to be full. A big bald man in an apron waived to Thomas as they walked in. He lead them to a small table in the middle of the room and beamed at Tony. "For very famous man we reserve table Mr Tony Hobbes."

They ate chicken and corn cakes and drank several bottles of the local beer. The owner had three sons and they took Ben out into the dusty, back yard to play football. There were soon many men crowded around the table asking Tony question after question about his life in Britain. Although this was far more hassle than he would have had in the hotel he didn't mind in the slightest. He just felt happy to at last be meeting some African people.

Time flew by and he was amazed when he looked at his watch and discovered that it was after eleven. He started to make his farewells and half an hour later he carried his sleepy son to the Land Rover.

When they got in he said, "Thanks for that Thomas.

We've had a great time. We have just over a week left here and I would like to do more of this. How do you suggest that we go about it?"

Thomas stared out of the window thoughtfully. "Maybe I could help Mr Tony."

"Go on."

"My Christmas holiday is start tomorrow. I am going home to see my family in Uganda. It is a very long journey. Many buses. If you want I can take you. These many buses would be too hard for the little boy. But if you hired a car the journey would not be so long. We could both drive. On the way I show you many beautiful places. When we get there you like my country very much. White men called my country 'The Pearl of Africa' because it is too beautiful. My village is in the East of Uganda, near to the mountains. You have never seen such mountains Mr Tony. They are called the 'Mountains of the Moon'."

Tony was staggered by the offer. "Wow. That sounds absolutely brilliant. My only worry is little Ben. You see, we came here to see animals."

Thomas grinned. "You no worry Mr Tony. My brother Samuel he is working as a warden in the National Park. It is called the Ruwenzori. There are very big forests there. He will take us there. He will show you the gorillas. There is no greater thing to see. This I make promise to you."

That was enough to make up Tony's mind up. The next morning was busy as he made arrangements. The tour leader was horrified to hear that his famous guest was leaving. Tony gave few details and never let anyone know where he was going in case it gave Thomas trouble when he returned to the hotel after Christmas. A little before lunchtime a hire company delivered a big Toyota 4x4 and Tony was off. He collected Thomas from the restaurant and they headed north.

Their journey took them three days but it was filled with magic. They passed the massive snowy peak of Mount Kenya. They saw the millions of pink flamingos on lake

Nakuru. They saw the small stream that was the source of the river Nile as it trickled out of Lake Victoria. They stopped at the airport in Kampala, the capital of Uganda, and Tony altered his flight home.

As they drove east for mile after mile Tony could only agree with Thomas. It was indeed a beautiful country. The towns and villages were run down and very poor but the people were friendlier than any he had ever met before. As they drove Thomas told him all about the village. His father was the local chief and so had to deal with all aspects of the life of the community. After two days Tony felt that he already knew many of the people as Thomas told tale after tale of the life of the village.

It was just after lunchtime on the third day when Thomas stopped the car and pointed to a cluster of thatched huts on top of a small hill. "This Mapote. This is my home."

As they parked up in the middle of the village children seemed to appear from nowhere and they danced around the vehicle. A tall, grave looking man came out of a hut that was rather bigger than the rest. His stern expression vanished as soon as he saw Thomas and he grinned.

Thomas said to Tony. "This is my father. He is our chief."

The rest of that day and the whole of the next day were endlessly busy. Thomas introduced Tony to everyone and took him around the coffee plantations that gave the people their living. Samuel, Thomas's brother arrived in the evening and agreed to take them to see the gorillas the next day. Tony smiled when he realised that the next day was Christmas Day. What a very odd way to spend a Christmas.

They were up well before dawn and they drove for four hours along small bumpy tracks, which climbed higher and higher into the mountains. As they drove, the forests of huge trees closed around them tighter and tighter. Every now and then they would reach a pass and the view would open up before them. Tony gasped at the astonishing scenery as the seemingly unending forests swept up to jagged snowy peaks.

At last they stopped at a small clearing with two huts. Samuel took them inside and told them that this was his home and his office. He made them tea and cooked eggs. A little after nine they started out and walked into the forest.

They walked and walked and walked. It was tough going as they had to clamber over roots and duck under vines. They stopped for five minutes every hour and drank tea from a flask. During the third halt Samuel tapped Tony on the shoulder and pointed to Ben. Ben had a look of complete wonder on his face and he was listening to the weird collection of bird sounds that echoed around the trees.

"Mr Tony. This boy is a young lion. For three hours we are walking very hard but he no complain. He is strong boy. You are proud father I think."

Tony looked at his son fondly. "Very proud."

"I think too that your leg must be feeling better now."

Tony was amazed. He hadn't even thought about his leg for days. Samuel was right. He had marched away for three hours and it didn't even ache. Now that was a good Christmas present.

Samuel became serious. "Now you must now listen to me good Mr Tony. Very soon we will come to the gorillas. They are good animals and they will do us no harm. They will only attack us if we make them frightened. When we get there the big male silverback will come and look at us. You must not move Mr Tony. You just stand very still and he will accept us."

After they had walked a further ten minutes they heard a tremendous crashing sound. It was the sound of big branches splitting. Samuel put his hand up and they walked very slowly.

And suddenly they were there. There were five of them. A huge silverback male, two smaller females and two babies. The silverback was simply enormous. Tony guessed that he must have weighed nearly 100 stone. He snapped a big thick branch off a tree and Tony could not believe his strength. As he munched away at the leaves on the branch he glanced over to them. Eventually he put down the branch and seemed mildly annoyed at having guests. He loped across to where they stood and sat down on a tree stump no more than six feet away.

Tony knew that he had never been half as frightened in his whole life. He tightened his grip on Ben's shoulder. Samuel spoke very softly. "It is OK. He just wants to see who we are. Just stand very still. You need not have fear Mr Ben."

When Ben spoke back his voice was quite normal. "I'm not frightened Sam". Tony didn't think that he could speak at all.

The silverback scratched and fidgeted for five minutes and then got bored with them and went and sat back down with his branch. He grunted to the two females who gave their visitors a quick look and then ignored them.

They stayed with the gorillas for over an hour and one of the babies even came over and felt Ben's hair. Its mother was not amused and soon dragged it away by the scruff of its neck.

As they made their way back to Samuel's hut Tony felt more exhilarated than he had ever felt before. To his amazement he realised that being handed the F.A. cup at Wembley in his old Liverpool days was nothing compared to what he had just experienced.

As they drove back out of the mountains Ben fell fast asleep. Tony's fantastic mood was spoilt as Samuel told him of the terrible dangers that the gorillas faced from poachers. The wardens did what they could, but the forests were so huge that it was impossible to keep the poachers away. If it continued, then the gorillas would soon die out.

When they arrived back at the village Ben never woke up as Tony lifted him out of the Toyota and carried him into the hut that they had been given. As he walked over to the Chief's hut he limped very slightly as his leg was starting to stiffen.

Christmas dinner was corn cakes, monkey meat and beer. Somewhere far away Partick were due to play away at Dundee the next day, but it seemed so far away as not to be real any more.

Tony soon found that his own eyes were growing heavy in the warm, smoky hut. He stood up and started to say goodnight to everyone. The chief gave Thomas a look and nodded to him.

Thomas cleared his throat and spoke very formally. "Mr Tony. My father he ask me to speak for him. He ask me to beg from you very big favour. Is it good that I should speak?"

"Of course." Said Tony and sat back down feeling slightly uneasy. Thomas continued.

"Tomorrow he is Boxing Day. It is a day when we have a tradition here in Mapote. Our next village is Misumba, over this way." Thomas pointed in a northerly direction. "On every Boxing Day there is a football match between the men of Mapote and the men of Misumba. Tony, my chief says that you are now a man of Mapote. He says you should play this game with the other men of Mapote. He says this is a good thing. He says it is a good thing because for many, many years the men of Mapote they never can win this game."

It was a tough decision. If he made his injury worse by playing in a game in the middle of Africa there would be real trouble. But then it occurred to Tony that if he did in fact make his leg worse there was absolutely no way that anyone at the club would ever know how. It was a big advantage to be so far in the middle of nowhere. These people had been wonderful to Ben and himself. The least that he could do was to play football with them. He was quite confident about his leg. It had stood up to the long hike in the jungle really well. It was time that he kicked a ball anyway.

"No problem Thomas. But listen, my leg is not right yet. I'll have to play in defence. Deep at the back. I can't afford to run around too much. If you'll take me as a defender then I'm with you."

The hut erupted with cheers at the news. As Tony made his way back to his own hut he realised that this was a big game for his new friends.

Chapter 6
Boxing Day in Misumba

The next day the whole village walked for two miles through the coffee plantations to the village of Misumba. It was clear to Tony that Misumba was a much larger village than Mapote. There was a real carnival atmosphere about the place. The whole population of the village had gathered around a small flat field, which was marked out as a pitch. There were two sets of goalposts, which were made from bamboo and roughly tied up with rope.

The people of Misumba were gathered along the far touchline. The air was filled with the smell of cooking as a pig was being roasted over an open fire. There were several drums and small boys beat out a throbbing rhythm. The Mapote villagers settled themselves down on the opposite touchline and some of the boys unstrapped the drums that they carried on their backs and started to beat them. Both sides competed in singing and dancing.

A very old Land Rover pulled up and a silver-haired white man got out. He was quite old and tanned dark from years in the African sun. He wore the collar of a priest.

He smiled warmly as he came over to the Chief and Tony. "Good morning to you Mr Hobbes. To be sure news travels fast in these parts. It would seem that Mapote might make a bit more of a game of it this year. I hope so. Misumba won 13 – 0 last year. Let me introduce myself. I'm Father O'Malley. I'm a missionary and they always get me to be the referee. I can't keep up with play as well as I once could but I like to think that the Good Lord helps me with my decisions."

He had a warm Irish voice and Tony liked him straight away. As the two teams made their way out onto the pitch Tony could see why Mapote had not won for so long. His team was a real mixture of old and young. Three of his fellow defenders must have been well into their 50's and two of the midfield could not have been much older than twelve.

This certainly was not the case with the Misumba team. The larger village certainly had a larger squad of players to chose from and most of their players seemed to be very fit looking young men in their twenties.

His fears were more than borne-out when the game started. The younger men of Misumba poured down on the ageing Mapote defence. Any hopes that Tony had of an easy morning stroll soon vanished. He was soon breathing hard as he had to throw himself into tackle after tackle to try and stop the constant Misumba attacks. He couldn't remember having to work so hard. His fellow players gave it absolutely everything but after twenty minutes their defence was at last broken and Misumba scored.

Every now and then when the ball flew over the bar and into the coffee bushes there was a chance to take a breather whilst the little boys raced to collect the ball. On these occasions Tony looked over to the touchline to check that Ben was OK. He saw that he was with a tall thin boy who was much paler than the other villagers were. He hadn't seen him before.

Ben had brought his football with him and he was laughing with delight as his new friend performed a series of tricks. After two more goals the ball once again was hoofed deep into the coffee and Tony once again watched the pale boy. He was tremendously clever with the ball, and he effortlessly juggled it from foot to foot, onto his head, onto the back of his neck, back to his foot. Tony couldn't help but whistle to himself as the boy kicked the ball high in the air, did a cartwheel, and collected it easily on his chest as it dropped.

At long last the half-time whistle was blown and the weary men of Mapote trudged back to their supporters whilst the Misumba team were greeted by drums and singing.

Tony wandered over to Ben. "You OK Ben?"

"I'm great Dad. This is my new friend Simon."

Tony shook the boy's hand. The boy said very formally. "It is a very big honour to meet you Mr Tony Hobbes. My name is Simon Matembo."

"Who are you supporting then Simon. Are you a Misumba man?"

"No Sir. I am here to support Mapote. I am of Mapote."

"That's strange." Said Tony. "We have never seen you in the village."

"No. This is true." The boy seemed uneasy. There was something strange about him. His skin was so much lighter than that of any of the other villagers and the shape of his face was different too. Tony was curious. "Why is that Simon?"

"It is how it must be sir. My mother and me live some distance from the village. We live a private life."

"Well why are you not playing Simon, you seem pretty skilful, I reckon that we could do with you. What is the problem? Do you not like playing in actual games?"

Simon's eyes flashed. "Why no sir. I love football. Football is my life."

Stranger and stranger. "Then why?" Asked Tony.

"Because it is best." Said the boy rather sadly.

At this point Father O'Malley came over. "Well Tony, uphill battle wouldn't you say?"

"Just a bit." Said Tony. "I'm just trying to persuade young Simon here to join us. He looks like he could give us another striking option." The priest's face darkened and he lead Tony to one side.

"I'd be careful Tony. You may open up a can of worms here. The Mapote men won't let Simon play."

"Why on earth not?"

O'Malley sighed. "Look Tony, it's a very long story. I'll tell it quickly. Years ago there was a young missionary from Scotland in Mapote. One day he found a young girl who had walked from the mountains. The poor thing was half-dead from starvation and he took her in. She recovered but the villagers were never happy. They said that she was a witch. She grew up at the mission house and he educated her. She grew into a beautiful young thing and then things went wrong. She became pregnant and the missionary fled back to Scotland. That is why Simon is such a light colour. The missionary was the father. His mother went to live in a hut about a mile from the village. The villagers don't dare drive her away. They are frightened that she would put a curse on them. But they have nothing to do with either her or her son."

Tony felt angry. "Come on Father, this is hocus pocus. I'm not having this."

"Be careful Tony."

"Careful nothing. Simon, come with me."

He marched over to where the other members of the team were catching their breath for the second half. "Thomas. It is time for a substitution. I've been watching this lad. I reckon he is just what we need up front."

Thomas looked appalled. "Mr Tony. Please, this is not a good thing. This boy he is not to play." The chief spoke fast to his son. Thomas translated. "Chief he say no. He say boy is no play. This must be Mr Tony."

Tony was livid. "Now you tell the chief this. If he has a problem because Simon here has a white daddy and a black mummy, then he has another problem. You see I have a black daddy and a white mummy. So if Simon can't play for Mapote, then neither can I."

This caused an outpouring of conversation. At last the chief, who was hugely troubled, gave his reluctant permission. Tony was delighted. He clapped Simon on the back. "OK my friend you're on. If you are as good on the pitch as you are at doing tricks we are still in this game."

The boy seemed both delighted and nervous.

O'Malley blew his whistle and they made their way back onto the pitch. There was a change in the mood when the Misumba supporters saw Simon line up in attack. The game started and it was more fast and furious than before. Tony saw that Simon was constantly being kicked and pushed when the referee was looking the other way. The worst culprit was a huge man who played in the Misumba defence.

When Misumba won a corner Tony decided to take some action. At the moment that the big defender jumped, Tony nudged him hard in the back with his shoulder and sent him crashing to the floor. The big man leapt to his feet and eyeballed Tony. Tony pushed his face in close. "Listen big man, you leave the kid alone or I'll have you, got that!"

O'Malley pulled them apart and tutted at Tony. Ten minutes into the second half Tony won the ball with a thumping tackle and looked up. He clipped a high ball forward for Simon to run on to. The boy collected the pass on his chest without slowing his run. He then nudged the ball over a defender's head with his right thigh and smashed the ball as it dropped with his left foot. The ball had never hit the ground and the boy had never broken his stride. The ball shot into the corner of the goal like a bullet. It was without doubt the finest piece of sheer skill that Tony had ever seen.

The goal was met by total silence either side of the pitch. Tony ran forward to congratulate Simon who was smiling happily. "Great goal son. Keep it going."

The other players completely ignored him. The pace of the game intensified. Simon was kicked time and again, and Tony found that he was playing harder and harder. Four more times he managed to find enough space in the wild pace of the match to hit telling through balls to Simon. On each occasion the boy scored with skill that was absolutely breathtaking.

At last O'Malley blew his whistle. Mapote had won 5 – 4. Yet there were no celebrations. Both sets of supporters simply packed up and made their way home. Thomas seemed guilty when he came over to Tony.

"Thank you Mr Tony. You played a fine game. My people should thank you as well. I am sorry that they are so rude."

"It's not me that they should thank." Said Tony. "It is young Simon. He won you the game."

Thomas shook his head. "He does not play real football. He is playing the devil's football. It was the bad spirits of the forest who were playing there Mr Tony."

"I'm sorry Thomas but I cannot believe that."

Thomas smiled sadly. "You must believe what you believe Mr Tony. I will go now."

O'Malley came over. "Well Tony you've made it a day to remember. Can I give you a lift?"

"No thanks Father. I'll walk the boy home. He looks like he needs some company." He looked over sadly to where Simon was sitting talking to Ben.

O'Malley smiled at him. "This is Africa Tony. There are many things that seem strange to us. At times we have tried to interfere when we maybe should have left things well alone. I have been here for 40 years, and I can promise you that there is nothing that you can do."

Tony looked at him evenly. "Ah but there is Father O'Malley, there is. You see, I believe that I have just played on the same pitch as one of the greatest talents on the planet. I'm not talking pretty good here. I'm talking Pele and Maradonna. Now I may not know much about African culture but I do know about football. I'm taking the boy away from here O'Malley. I'm taking him back to Scotland and I'll make sure that he gets what he deserves. And God help anyone who tries to stop me."

Chapter 7
Persuasion

Tony and Simon talked together quietly as they made their way back through the coffee plantations to Mapote. When they were about a quarter of a mile from the village they turned onto a small path which wound its way up the side of a hill. After a few hundred yards they came to the top where a single hut stood looking down on the plantations below.

The hut was neat and well-maintained and it was surrounded by colourful garden of flowers. At one side of the hut there was a large vegetable garden where a young woman was working at pulling up weeds. She sang softly to herself as she worked, and the sound of her voice coupled with the light breeze, which was rustling the trees, gave Tony a huge sense of tranquillity.

She turned and smiled as Simon spoke to her.

"Mother, please allow me to introduce you to my new friends. This is Mr Tony and his son Mr Ben. They are here visiting Mapote. They are from Scotland."

She wiped the dusty soil from her hands and smiled warmly as she greeted them. Tony was knocked back by her beauty which was spectacular. She seemed to be little more than 30 years old which meant that she must have been very young when she had given birth to Simon.

She pulled up some home-made stools and they sat in front of the hut whilst a pot of water came to the boil. Tony was very impressed by the dazzling array of flowers, which grew all around him.

"I must congratulate you on your garden Mrs Matembo, it is truly beautiful."

"Why thank you, gardening has always been a passion to me. Now please, you must both call me Rose, you see, I am even named after a flower."

"Also, I must say that your English is exceptional. I was wondering how it was that Simon spoke the language so well, now I can see why."

Her eyes became slightly sad and distant. "Well, I had a very good teacher, but that was a long, long time ago. I'm glad to know that it has stood the test of time."

She made coffee and they talked. Tony was impressed at the way that she brought Ben into the conversation and listened to him carefully. It was in fact Ben who described the match with Misumba, which he did which great relish. Tony smiled as his desperate exploits in the centre of the Mapote defence paled into insignificance when compared to Simon's spectacular goals. Rose was delighted and said,

"I'm so pleased. Simon spends hours and hours with his football, it is so nice that he has been able to play in a real game."

She prepared lunch and told them a little of their life at the top of the hill. She showed an amazing lack of bitterness towards the villagers who had excluded herself and her son. They lived a very simple, quiet life.

When lunch was finished Tony asked Simon if he would take Ben for a look round. Simon agreed readily and the two boys went away. Tony took a deep breath and decided to begin. He knew that what he was about to do was going to be tough.

"Tell me Rose, how much do you know about football?"

She shook her head. "Very little I'm afraid. As you can guess, we are isolated here. We know little of what goes on in the outside world. Tell me please, it is of interest."

Tony explained about the massive explosion that Football had seen all over the world. He told of World Cups and massive shiny stadiums packed with supporters. He told of the newspapers and the television and the new supporters' megastores. At times her mouth opened in wonder when he told her of the price of tickets or replica shirts.

She nearly fell off her stool when he told her of how much he had earned when he was a Liverpool player. This made her thoughtful. "Tell me Mr Tony. Can this be right? Can it be right for a man to earn such riches for playing a game when there are so many who are hungry?"

Tony shook his head. "Since I have been in Uganda I have thought of little else Rose. What can I say? Of course it is not right, but then there is an awful lot that is wrong with the world."

They were silent for a while. At last she spoke. "Mr Tony there is something that you want to say to me but you lack the courage. Please do not be afraid. I am but a poor woman and I will do you no harm. The people of Mapote credit me with all sorts of powers but, alas, I do not possess them."

Tony took a deep breath. "Rose, I have been a professional footballer since I was seventeen years old. That is sixteen years. I have played my game at the very highest level. I have played in the World Cup finals and I have been lucky enough to play against the best players on earth." He paused and chose his words with care. "However I saw the greatest of them all playing this morning in

Misumba. Your son is not simply a good footballer, he is exceptional, one in ten million. His talent is greater than anything that I have ever seen. I would like to take him to Scotland so that he can use his talent to the full.

"I could tell you of the fame that he will know and the vast sums of money that he will earn, but these things are not what is most important. What is most important is that such an exceptional talent should not be wasted."

She sighed as he spoke these words. "Of course you are right Mr Tony. Simon is now nearly a man. I have always known that the time must come when he must leave me. It is hard for any mother; maybe you can see that it is particularly hard for me. But I would never stand in his way. But you must tell me more. Where will he live? How will he eat? Where will he find the warm clothes that he will need in such a cold country?"

"He will stay with me. I have a wife called Karen and I promise that we will be like mother and father to him. I guarantee that I would never allow any harm to come to Simon any more than I would allow it to come to Ben."

She looked deep into his face and was very quiet. "I see that this is true. I feel that you are a good man Mr Tony. I feel that I may trust you with my son. I will show you something."

She disappeared into the hut for a few minutes and then came out with two envelopes. "Do you know anything of my history, Mr Tony?"

"A little, Father O'Malley told me some."

"He is a good man. He visits me sometimes. He will have told you that it was a fellow missionary who is Simon's father. He was a good man too. I loved him. When he found that I was pregnant he could not bear the shame and he ran away. I do not blame him for this for he was only young. Sometimes we receive letters from him. He is now a priest in a place called Kirkcaldy. Sometimes he sends money, twice he has sent these."

She passed the two envelopes to Tony. Inside were two British passports both made out in the name of Simon Matembo. She continued. "He sent the first one a year after he left this place. The second one came ten years later when the first expired. I believe that one of your worries must have been a passport. Well as you can see, you have no need to worry after all."

Again she paused and gazed sadly over the endless green hills. "You may take my son Mr Tony. He is lucky to have found a man like you."

Simon and Ben joined them a few minutes later and Ben rattled on happily about some birds that they had seen on their walk.

When Ben had finished Rose said to her son. "Simon. Mr Tony has something to say to you and you must listen carefully. He has talked to me about this thing and I agree with what he says."

Simon looked at Tony with interest. Tony started his speech. "Simon, I have seen many, many footballers in my life, but none of them are as good as you. God has given you a great talent. I would like you to come with Ben and me to Scotland. You will live with us in our home. I will take you to play for my old club, Queens Park. I will help you to become one of the greatest players in the world. I promise that I will always be with you. You will never be alone."

Ben leapt off his stool and shrieked with joy. "Oh Simon, this is great, you will have the room next to mine, and I will show you my computer and my bike and everything."

But Simon did not leap for joy. His big eyes filled with tears and he fought hard not to let them fall. "Mr Tony, you are very kind, but I must say no. I told you that football is my life. This is nearly true, but it is not my life. I would love more than anything to come with you to Scotland. But I cannot. I cannot leave my mother alone with these people who say that she is a witch. I have spoken now. It must not be."

Both Rose and Tony tried to change his mind but neither was able to. At last he stood up from the stool and spoke to his mother. "Mother, now I am seventeen years old. I am a man now. You can not tell me what to do. I will not leave."

He started to walk away very slowly. Tony shouted after him. "Simon, I will sort things out. I promise. I will be back soon."

The boy never turned his head as he walked away.

Four days later they were back home in Glasgow. Karen's eyes were wide as Ben recounted their many adventures. She kept looking over to Tony with a questioning look on her face. On each occasion he gave a small smile and nodded. Later, when Ben at last ran out of steam and went to bed, Tony and Karen sat together in the lounge. She leaned her head on his shoulder and said. "I go to Africa and we have a simple week on the beach, and then as soon as the pair of you are out of my sight, well, I can barely believe it. What adventures!"

He chuckled. "What adventures indeed. We certainly had a fair old time."

"Tell me about Simon."

He told her and tried to put in words the magic of the young man's ability. He tried to explain the impact that Africa had made on him and how he had to find a way to help the gifted young Ugandan.

She thought about what he said. "So you will be going back?"

"I must."

"But what else can you say? What can make him change his mind? Should you change his mind? After all, think how it would be for his mother."

He groaned. "I know, I know, I know. I thought of nothing else all the way home on the plane. I don't know what to do, but I have to do something."

She brightened. "Well I know what you have to do and I am amazed that it hasn't occurred to you."

"What?"

"You need to talk to your dad. If anyone can sort this out, then my guess is that it is Winston."

A slow smile spread over Tony's face. "You're absolutely right. Of course. Dad will know what to do."

He drove round to his father's house the next evening. To start with Winston was delighted to hear that his son had left the official tour and had gone to find the real Africa. He was fascinated to hear about the Boxing Day match but became suspicious when Tony said that he needed his help. When Tony said that he was going back to try and bring Simon over he was appalled.

"Boy, you've gone clean out of your head. How can you say that this boy is that good? This is madness."

"Dad, have I ever given you a lecture on Union Law?"

"Of course not."

"Then please do not try to tell me about football. I tell you, Simon is a world beater, you just have to believe me."

Winston grunted. "Well I accept that. So what help do you want from me?"

"Come with me when I go back. You'll work something out. You know what these villages are like, it is like Barbados."

The big man nearly exploded. "Boy you are crazy. I don't have some easy, lazy job like you! I can't just go swannin' off to Africa to persuade some young boy to be a footballer! I'm just a simple dock worker, I can't go payin' no fancy air fares."

"Come on dad, you haven't taken a holiday in years and I'm paying. Come on man, show some spirit."

The argument raged for two hours more, but after half an hour Tony knew that he had hooked his prey. When his father at last agreed to join him in a return trip, he started to grill him mercilessly about every aspect of life in the village of Mapote.

A little after midnight he told his son of his plan. By one in the morning the plan was agreed. Three weeks later they sat next to each other as their plane touched down at Jinja airport on the outskirts of Kampala.

Chapter 8
The Big Chief of the Clyde

Winston and Tony spent a busy day and a half shopping in Kampala and they made several more stops on the road east to Mapote. Tony was amazed at the ease with which his father dropped into the rhythm of African life. Within a matter of minutes the big man dominated every market place or restaurant that they visited.

When they were about five miles from Mapote they stopped the small lorry that they had hired and Winston got changed. His jeans and sweatshirt were packed away. He replaced them with a long white robe, which he tied around his waist with a bright red sash. He hung a large gold chain around his neck. He grinned at Tony. "Well boy, how do I look?"

"Like a dog's dinner to be honest."

Tony had been far from convinced about the outfit that his father had insisted on wearing, but Winston had said that it was vital that he made a big impression. As he looked his father up and down he couldn't help but agree that he would definitely make an impression. His father tapped his head comically and said. "I nearly forgot. There is one more item."

He rummaged in his bag and pulled out a thick varnished walking stick with a flourish. Tony groaned.

Twenty minutes later Tony parked up the truck in front of the Chief's hut. The villagers poured out to see who had come to visit. Several grinned happily when they recognised Tony. They all gasped in astonishment as Winston slowly stepped out of the passenger door. Tony was both delighted and relieved when he saw Samuel come out of his father's hut. Without Samuel, finding a translator would have been difficult.

Winston stood up to his full six and a half feet and said in a commanding voice. "Show me where I can find the chief of this place. Tell him that I have been sent from far away. Tell him that I come from The Big Chief of the Clyde himself. Tell him that the Big Chief of the Clyde sends him messages and gifts."

Samuel's eyes nearly popped out and he scuttled back into the hut to fetch his father. When the Chief came out Winston gave him an elaborate bow and again spoke in a loud voice.

"I bring you greetings from the Great Chief of the Clyde. This is a Chief who is so great that beside him I am as small as a mouse."

The watching crowd gasped as Samuel translated. Any man who made the giant in the white robe look as small as a mouse must be a great man indeed. Winston continued. "My boy here has told my Chief all about the great people of Mapote. He has told of many things. My Chief has sent me with many messages. But before I give these messages he has ordered me to bring a great feast. Tony, open the back of the truck."

Tony, who was finding it terribly difficult to keep a straight face, opened the back of the truck. Inside were chickens, three pigs, many crates of beer, and a whole host of other foods that they had bought in Kampala. A cheer went up from the villagers when they saw the contents of the truck and within minutes they had started to prepare the feast.

Whilst fires were lit and tables were pulled out, Winston and Tony sat with Samuel and the Chief in front of the hut. Winston sat bolt upright on his stool with his hands laid one over the other on his stick. He said little; he merely watched the preparations being made in front of him with a face like stone. Young children crept up to look at him more closely, and one was even brave enough to reach out and touch his stick. Winston never moved a muscle.

THE BIG CHIEF OF THE CLYDE

Three hours later darkness had fallen and the huge banquet was prepared. The Chief rose to his feet and waved for silence. Samuel translated for Winston and Tony.

"We welcome our visitors. We welcome Mr Tony and his father, the representative of The Great Chief of the Clyde. We thank this Great Chief for the feast he has brought. We will listen to his message."

The Chief sat and Winston slowly drew himself up to his full height. He paused for a long moment, then stared his speech.

"My Chief is a very great man. He rules a very great kingdom. His kingdom is called Glasgow. It sits on the mighty river Clyde and it is far, far away. My Chief has listened to my son Tony. My son Tony came back from Mapote and he told my Chief many things. But it is only one thing that made my Chief send me all this way to see you."

Again a long, long pause. The tension was electric.

"Tony told my Chief about a boy called Simon Matembo. He said that this boy was a great footballer. For my Chief, football is more important than all other things. My Chief asked Tony 'Why is it that you come back to me and you leave this Simon Matembo in Africa'. My Chief was very angry at Tony. He yelled and shouted at Tony.

HOW DARE HE COME HOME
WITHOUT THIS SIMON MATEMBO!"

Winston's voice hit a new note and his audience shook with fear. Small children hid behind their parents as he stared hard at his audience.

"Tony, he tremble before the rage of my Chief. He told my chief that this boy would not come when he was asked. He told him that the people of Mapote say that his mother is a witch. He say that this boy will never leave his mother alone with people like these. When he hears this my chief loses his anger. He say to Tony that it is not his fault. He say to Tony that this Simon Matembo must be a good boy because he will not leave his mother. He forgive Tony now. Then he speaks to me. He tells me to go and see those people of

Mapote. He says I must bring feast for you. He says I must offer you great gifts."

Again a pause.

"Why does he offer these gifts? Because he wants this boy Simon Matembo to play football in his Kingdom? What must you do for me to deliver these gifts? You must allow this boy's mother to come to Mapote and not call her a witch any more. This is what he has said. This woman is an educated woman. My Chief will pay for her to go to Kampala to learn to become a teacher. Whilst she is in Kampala he will build a fine school here in Mapote. This school will have a big football pitch. This school will have a satellite dish and a television to bring pictures from the sky. These pictures will show you this boy Simon Matembo and my boy Tony when they play football.

"When the school is built this lady Rose Matembo will come back from Kampala and she will be the teacher for the children of Mapote. And the teacher will live in a fine hut in the village of Mapote. And the people of Mapote will show respect to the teacher.

"These are the words of my chief. These are the gifts of my chief. You must now decide these things."

Winston sat down on the stool and once again became a statue. Almost immediately a loud discussion broke out among the villagers of Mapote. The argument raged for over an hour and many longed for it to be finished so that they could start the feast. At last the Chief once again stood and waved for silence.

"We have listened to the message from The Great Chief of the Clyde. We have heard what he has said. We will do this thing that he asks. The boy Simon Matembo may go and play football in the Kingdom of the Great Chief of the Clyde. The woman Rose Matembo will be our teacher and she will live amongst us with our respect. It is spoken."

Winston again rose and held out a hand to the chief. The chief winced at the hardness of Winston's grip. Winston said, "Tomorrow I will come with you to tell these things to Rose Matembo. Now we eat the feast."

The feast went on long into the night and the next morning there were many sore heads in the village of Mapote. Tony, Samuel, Winston and the Chief made their way up the path to the hut at the top of the hill. The chief seemed rather worse for wear, but Winston was once again resplendent in his white robe.

It was hard to say what came as the greatest shock to Simon and Rose as they came out of their hut. Maybe it was the surprise at seeing Tony again. Maybe it was the even bigger surprise at seeing the chief of Mapote and his son at their door. Probably it was the sight of the giant man in the white robe. Tony stepped forward quickly and said. "Hello Rose, Hello Simon" and he winked at them both.

Winston said. "Miss Rose Matembo. The Chief has things he would like to say to you. We will wait whilst he says these things."

The chief made his speech and Samuel translated for the benefit of Tony and Winston. The astonishment spread over the faces of Simon and his mother. At the end of his speech the chief bowed slightly. There was a silence. Tony looked to Simon. "I promised to do what I could. Will you come now?"

Simon was about to speak but his mother beat him to it. "He will go or I will never speak to him again."

As they talked Samuel guided Tony away from the group. As they looked down at the village below he said. "It is a wonderful thing that you have done Mr Tony. Many of us younger people have felt bad about what has happened. I and my brother Thomas have felt bad for many years. It is the older men who have made up these stories. One day when I am Chief I would have stopped this thing. I am glad that I do not now have to wait. Rose will be fine in Mapote now. The spell is broken. The spell was the foolishness of old men."

In the afternoon Tony and Winston collected Simon and his mother and they drove over to see Father O'Malley. The news of the events of the evening before had already reached him and there was a twinkle in his eye as he led them into his small house.

"Well I've been hearing all manner of colourful stories this morning. I've heard of a giant in white sent to Mapote by the Great Chief of the Clyde. I gather that must be your good self – Mr Hobbes. Well, it's a pleasure to meet you." O'Malley noticed Winston's slightly embarrassed expression. "Now go away with you Mr Hobbes. Don't be embarrassed with me. I always say that the Lord moves in mysterious ways. I don't care what you did so long as you've got the old men of Mapote to drop this ridiculous business."

O'Malley agreed to make all the arrangements to send Rose to teaching college in Kampala. He also agreed to act as a banker and gave Tony details of his account in the capital. Tony said that he would send the money for the school and Rose's fees in installments as and when O'Malley requested them. When all the arrangements were completed he smiled at Tony.

"It's a lot of money Tony. You're a generous man."

"Not at all. Once I get Simon here playing for Scotland I will pay all the bills out of my win bonuses."

"I'll believe you if you like," The old priest chuckled, "But I promise you that it isn't a sin for a footballer to have a heart."

The next morning Simon said a tearful goodbye to his mother and the three of them set off for Kampala. Once again when they were a few miles down the road Winston pulled up and changed. Simon looked on wide-eyed as the big man climbed back into the cab wearing his jeans and a T-shirt. Winston clapped him on the back merrily.

"Don't look so worried boy. I had to put on a bit of an act to get those old men to see a bit of sense. Underneath the fancy white robe I'm just an ordinary sort of guy."

"Ha!" Snorted Tony. "Don't believe a word of it Simon. He's an absolute tyrant."

Chapter 9
Back in the kingdom of the Clyde

It was a busy time for everyone as the three men arrived back in Scotland at the beginning of February. Tony decided to be guided by Karen as to the pace they should set for Simon to settle in. For a week they simply drove him around and showed him the sights. It was almost too much for Simon to take in. Before coming to Glasgow, the biggest town that he had ever been to was the dusty little settlement at Kabale, and he had only ever been there three times.

He seemed to never lose a look of utter astonishment at everything that he saw. The only thing that did not enchant him was the weather, and even with three coats on he still shivered. Ben was delighted to see him again and after a few days he was well on the way to turning Simon into a fellow computer-addict.

Tony made an appointment and went to see the Headmaster at the local High School. Initially the Head was most apologetic, but he said that it would be quite impossible for him to accept a pupil to do Highers if he had never sat Standard Grade. Tony pointed out that the boy had been very well-educated, but it was still deemed impossible. Tony then pointed out that the boy was an exceptional footballer, and he could well help the school to success in the up coming Glasgow Schools Championships and the Head felt that there just might be something that he could do. Tony then hinted that if the Head could find a place for Simon, he would personally be willing to come down after school on Thursdays to help coach the school team and the Head seemed quite sure that a place could be found.

Simon started school the following Monday. Karen smiled fondly as she watched him make his way inside looking tremendously smart in his new uniform. She had taken several pictures and mailed them to his mother. "Just imagine." She said. "First day at school and he's seventeen!"

"He's settling in well don't you think love?"

She squeezed his arm. "Oh he's fine Tony. The lad's had a hard tough life and it's standing him in good stead. I tell you, there won't be much that will bother young Simon. He's made from hard bark."

Simon did indeed settle well in his new school over the next fortnight and he was clearly delighted with his new life in Scotland. Tony received more good news when he was given a clean bill of health to resume training. He played two reserve games and, although his touch was a bit out, he was well pleased with his general level of fitness. The leg held up fine and neither game was nearly as demanding as the Boxing Day battle in Misumba.

Partick were still not having the best of seasons and with only 10 games of the season to go they were hovering dangerously close to the relegation zone. The manager watched Tony come through his third reserve game and collared him after the game.

"Well Tony, that all seemed to go OK. What do you think? Ready?"

"Yeah boss. Nae bother. Lets get ourselves up the table a bit shall we?"

Simon was ecstatic when Tony told him that he would be playing the following Saturday. Partick were playing away at Hearts who were in the middle of a fine run of matches that had carried them to third in the league. As the players underwent their preparations in the dressing-room Tony was alarmed by the lack of confidence that filled the room. Things had certainly gone a long way down hill in his absence.

The first ten minutes were a nightmare. Hearts flew at them like men possessed. The crowd bayed for blood. They hit the post and seemed to have a perfectly good goal disallowed. Partick hung on. Whenever they won the ball they hoofed it away up the field.

After 25 minutes play was held up due to a clash of heads. Tony waved several of the players over to him. They stood breathing deeply.

"OK, that's it. You all seem to have forgotten how to play football but I haven't. You're like a bunch of ten-year-olds. What the hell do you think is going on? No more hoofing. From now on we get the ball and we keep it. Make them chase for it. They can't keep up this pace forever. The next bloke who hoofs away possession will have me to deal with. GOT IT!"

They all nodded eagerly. When play resumed a vastly different Partick took shape. Tony started to pull all the strings. The noise from the stands eased and then went quiet.

Tony felt a confident energy surge through him. Every pass found its mark. Twice the Hearts midfield tried to take him down and on both occasions he jinked out of the way with ease. He couldn't remember playing better.

In the 43rd minute he collected the ball in the centre circle and sensed that there was space ahead of him. The pace of the game was obviously beginning to tell on his marker. He burst forward into the space. The centre half was drawn out to meet him and he slipped the ball just before he could make the tackle. He hurdled the sliding legs and ran on to meet the return pass. He looked up and saw Billy McKie making a run to the back post. He clipped the ball over and Bobby gleefully headed it in. They both ran to salute the rejoicing Partick Fans behind the goal and Tony spotted Simon leaping around with joy next to his father.

The goal had an immediate effect. The dressing-room at half-time was an altogether different place. It was almost as if a completely different side ran out for the second half. All of a sudden the ball was fizzing around the pitch. The second goal came as no surprise. Tony was substituted with fifteen minutes to go. As he trotted from the pitch the small bunch of travelling fans chanted "Hobbo! Hobbo!" He grinned and clapped his hands over his head. He was back.

When he met up with Simon after the game the boy was nearly beside himself with excitement.

"Mr Tony that was fantastic. I never knew that football could be like this. The stadium is so huge. And the people! So many people. I would never have believed that so many people would come to watch a football game. How many were there? Hundreds. Thousands. And the noise! I have never heard so much noise! And Mr Tony, they all love you. They sing your name . . ."

Tony had to put his hands up to stem the flow from the young African. "Hey, hey, slow down. You're getting me out of breath just listening." He chuckled to himself.

"What is it Mr Tony?"

"Oh nothing really. It's just what you're saying about all the people and all the noise."

"Is this funny?"

"No, sorry, not really. It's just that you have so much to learn Simon. There were just over eight thousand people watching today and they made a little bit of noise. Next Sunday you will find out what real noise is all about."

"Why? Where are we going Mr Tony."

Tony smiled. "We are going to Ibrox to see the Old Firm Match."

The boy's eyes widened. "I have heard of this Old Firm Match. Everybody is talking about it at school. Is it true that it is such a big match?"

"Oh yes. It's all true. They don't come any bigger."

"But Mr Tony, how is it that we have got tickets. At school all the boys say it is not possible to get tickets for this game."

"Well being captain of Scotland does have a few perks you know."

Simon turned to Ben. "This is wonderful little Ben. I cannot wait to see this. I cannot believe that it is possible for there to be more people watching than there were here today. Are you excited too little Ben?"

Ben turned to his father with an imploring look in his eyes. "Can I Dad?"

Tony shook his head quickly. "No son, not yet."

Ben's face fell. Simon seemed confused. He turned to Winston. "And you Mr Winston. Will you be coming?"

Winston made a grumpy "Hummpff" sort of noise and shook his head angrily.

Now Simon was really confused. He turned again to Tony. "Mr Tony, if this game is so special why is it that you will not allow Little Ben to go? Why is it that Mr Winston does not go?"

Tony started to speak and then stopped. "I'm afraid it all takes a bit of explaining Simon. Let's leave it for now and get ourselves a McDonalds. Don't worry, I'll explain it all before we go."

As they made their way to the car he said to himself under his breath. "Well, at least I'll try to."

The next morning it was Tony's turn to be a spectator. Simon was making his debut for the school against Holyrood Secondary School. Holyrood had more or less ruled Glasgow football for many years and they had not been beaten for well over a season. On the other hand Highfield, Simon's new school, had no great reputation on the football field. The games between the two schools were generally painfully one sided.

There was a stir of excitement among the watching parents when Tony took his place on the touchline with Ben. Several boys ran over to get his autograph and he was signing when he heard a voice behind him.

"Hello Hobbo." When he turned he was amazed to see that it was Jim McCaig. McCaig had been the hard man of the Rangers midfield when Tony had first played at Ibrox when he was nineteen. Tony had ended that particular game bruised from head to toe and much wiser than when he had started. McCaig had come to the dressing-room after the match to invite him for a drink. Later in the bar the tough little midfielder had told Tony that he had done well and should go far. "I kicked you as hard as I know how and you still never went down and whinged. You're all right Tony." He had said in his thick accent. Tony had always liked McCaig.

"Jimmy! Long time no see. What are you doing here? I thought your lad was all grown up now."

"He is." Said McCaig. "I'm working Tony. Rangers have hired me as a scout. There are a couple of lads here that we're looking at. More to the point, what are you doing here? Have they got you scouting now?"

"No" Laughed Tony. "I have a friend of the family who is playing his first game. Me and Ben thought we would give him a bit of support."

"Good on you. Mind if I stand with you?"

"Course not. It will be good to catch up."

As the game kicked-off a thin rain started to fall. Holyrood got the ball and started to pass it around with a confident ease. Highfield chased it half-heartedly. It was rather like watching a cat teasing a wounded mouse. Then Simon darted back from the centre circle and nicked the ball off one of the midfielders. He danced through four tackles and chipped the ball delicately into the top corner of the

Holyrood net. His new classmates mobbed him whilst the Holyrood players looked at each other in amazement.

McCaig was transfixed. "I suppose that boy is the friend of the family Tony."

Tony grinned. "Sure is."

"And I suppose that he has an agent?"

"Sure has."

"And I suppose that is agent is your dad?"

"Right again."

"Mmmmm." McCaig never said another word as Simon went on to score eight goals in the first half. He didn't score any in the second half as he concentrated on setting up chances for his team-mates. Highfield won 12 – 3.

McCaig turned to Tony as the boys left the pitch. "He's special Tony. I mean Georgie Best special."

"I know."

"Make sure that you look after him."

"Don't worry. I will."

Chapter 10
New recruit

After training the next day Tony made the short trip across Glasgow to Hampden Park. He parked up and made his way to John Craig's office. He and Craig had been contemporaries in the Queens Park side sixteen years earlier. Unlike Tony, John had never made the step up to full time pro football. Instead he had gone to college and qualified as a P.E. teacher. During the school holidays he had taken his S.F.A. License Diploma and had landed his first Manager's job at Queens Park two years before. There were already whispers in the corridors of Scottish football that here was a young manager to watch out for.

Tony tapped on the door.

"Come in!" Craig's face broke into a huge smile when he saw Tony. "Well I never. This is some surprise. OK Hobbo, let me guess. You're fed up with pro football, fed up with the Premier League rat race, and so you've decided to chuck it all in and be an amateur again? Yeah? Well that's not a problem; you've come to the right place. You're in the team for Saturday."

Tony grinned. "Well it sounds tempting but there's still life in the old dog yet. I think I'll keep drawing the pay-cheques for as long as I can. Anyway John, how are things with you?"

"Fine. Can't complain. We've a cracking crop of youngsters coming through. Still not quite filling the stadium though."

Tony chuckled. Queens Park played at Hampden Park, the Scottish National Stadium, which had a capacity of in excess of 50,000. The average gate attracted to watch a Queen's Park game in the Third Division was generally a little over 500. Tony sat down and crossed his legs. "I keep hearing good things John. There's a bit of talk about you being the next Sir Alex Ferguson."

This time it was John Craig's turn to chuckle. "No chance of that. I'm not nearly grumpy enough."

"There's plenty of time John. Make sure you practise your moody look in the mirror every morning. Then you can work on chucking a few tea cups around at breakfast, and you'll be there in no time."

Craig got up and made a couple of coffees and sat back down. "Come on then Hobbo, to what do I owe this pleasure if you're really not going to sign for us."

"Are you still training in the evenings John?"

"Sure." A small grin was playing on Craig's face. He was becoming intrigued.

"How about I bring a lad down tomorrow night for you to have a look at."

"You DO know how many times I get asked this don't you?"

Tony smiled. "One heck of a lot I guess."

"Seriously. You wouldn't believe it. My mobile never stops ringing. But I assume you feel it should be different this time."

"Of course it's different. This is your Scotland captain speaking. Besides, we're mates."

Craig smiled. "OK, point taken. So what is this? A favour for a neighbour?"

"No. I wouldn't embarrass you like that. Let's just put it this way. I think this lad might just help you fill the Stadium up a bit."

Now Craig was really intrigued. "Go on Hobbo. What's the story?"

"No story today. You have a look at the lad tomorrow and then we'll talk."

"Fair enough. I'll see you about half past seven then."

Tony reached across to shake his old team-mate's hand. "Thanks John. I appreciate it."

NEW RECRUIT

The next evening Tony and Simon drove across the city. There were looks of surprise as they walked over to where the players were gathered. It certainly wasn't every day that the captain of the National team turned up at a Queens Park training session. Many of the younger players seemed quite star-struck

Craig blew his whistle and gathered all the players around him. "OK lads, you all know Hobbo here I'm sure. He's brought this young man along for a quick trial"

"Evening lads. Meet a pal of mine. This is Simon Matembo. Be nice to him won't you." Said Tony

To start with the players took Tony literally. They thought that Simon must have been the son of a friend or neighbour or something and they took care to give him space. When he scored his second goal they got the message. This was no rich kid being given the red carpet treatment. This was a serious trial.

For twenty minutes they tried all they could to tackle him. On the odd occasion they managed it. Most of the time they didn't. Simon scored two more goals and showed the full range of his breathtaking skills. When Craig blew his whistle they all looked on with complete astonishment.

Simon trotted over to Tony who said. "Good effort lad." Then to the other players. "Thanks boys."

Simon grinned from ear to ear. "Thank you all for the game. I enjoyed it very much."

They went over to the manager who was looking very thoughtful indeed. Another older man had joined him. Tony looked carefully and was delighted when he recognised John Craig's father. Don Craig had been a great midfielder for Rangers in the 1960's and had played for Scotland many times.

Tony shook his hand warmly. "Hello again Mr Craig. It's been a long time."

Don smiled. "Aye it has to be sure. Last time I watched you were a snotty little kid who couldn't kick his way out of a wet paper bag. You've done nae bad since then Tony."

"Aye. Nae bad. What brings you down here tonight?"

"John gave me a call. Told me about your visit. Got me a bit interested." He looked Simon up and down and shook the boy's hand and said. "I'm pleased to meet you Simon."

In a formal voice Simon replied. "For me it is indeed the very greatest honour sir."

John Craig glanced quickly to Tony. "A strange accent, where are you from Simon?"

"I am from Mapote. It is in Uganda. But I have a passport for the United Kingdom. I live with Mr Tony now."

The boy's manners made the two men smile. "How do you like Scotland Simon?"

"It is wonderful. I am very happy. Glasgow is my new home."

Tony said. "You best go and get changed now Simon. I'll be over in a minute"

They watched as the young African loped away.

John Craig spoke first. "I think he has just come through the trial Tony. When do you want him to start?"

"Why not next week. Reckon he'll get a game?"

The young manager chuckled. "Are you kidding, he'll go straight into the first team. But we need to sort a few things out first Tony."

"Like?"

"Like the fact that my phone is going to ring off the wall after about three matches. What's the state of play?"

"Oh I see." Tony was thoughtful for a moment. He hadn't thought this far ahead. "This is a rather unusual situation John. I found the lad in the back end of nowhere when me and Ben were on holiday in Africa at Christmas."

Craig's eyes widened. Tony continued. "Yeah, I know. Some story. Anyway I made his mum a lot of promises. We agreed that for the next few years school has to come first, no matter what. He should have another couple of years at school and then maybe he will want to go on to college.

"That's why I brought him to you John. Queen's Park is perfect for him. He can learn all the ropes while staying as an amateur and getting on with his studies. So if you get any approaches just pass them on to my dad. He'll be with Queen's Park for a year or two at least."

At this point Craig senior laughed loudly. "So Winston is the lad's agent is he?"

"Aye," said Tony.

"I pity the poor devil who has to negotiate that particular contract!" He then spoke in a rather wistful voice. "When I was eighteen years old Rangers went down to Manchester to play in a Testimonial match against United. It was 1963. They had a young lad called George Best playing. I haven't seen anyone like him for 30 years. Until this evening. You've got an eye Tony. This one is special. I mean really special. You do know how careful you will have to be don't you?"

"Go on."

Don shook his head sadly. "I've seen what happens if things go wrong Tony. I saw it close up with Slim Jim Baxter. We all know what happened to Georgie Best. Everyone is going to want a piece of him. He will need protecting. Really protecting."

Tony nodded. "I know. We're not going to allow any media near him for a while. We'll manage it I think. Well, my dad will. He'll be OK you know. He's had one heck of a hard life over in Uganda and it will stand him in good stead. But I take on board what you are saying."

The following Sunday afternoon Tony and Simon pulled on their coats ready to set off for the Old Firm game at Ibrox. The day before Tony had completed the full 90 minutes as Partick had convincingly beaten Kilmarnock 2 – 0 at home. His leg hadn't troubled him a bit and he had felt in tremendous form. Ben tried his best to put on a brave face but without much success. Tony bent down and ruffled his son's hair. "Come on Ben, chin up. Your time will come; you just have to wait for a while. OK?"

"Yes Dad."

"See if you can spot us in the crowd on the Tele."

Once they were in the car Simon started to question Tony. "Mr Tony. Are the people at this match really so bad that you do not allow little Ben to go there. Even Mr Winston will not go to this place."

Tony drummed his fingers on the steering wheel for a moment as he waited for a set of traffic lights to change to green. "Don't get me wrong Simon, it's not that the people are bad. No, it's not that at all. It's just that they behave badly. They get too excited."

"But Mr Tony, isn't this how it should be? People should be excited at a football match."

"Well yes, of course they should. Absolutely. But it isn't just the football that gets the fans going at an Old Firm Match. It's other stuff as well."

Simon frowned. "Other stuff? There will be more than football to see today?"

"No, not like that. No, it's just a football match. When I say other stuff I mean religion."

Simon frowned even more. "Religion? This is very strange Mr Tony. I was always taught that people went to a church for religion. Is it different here in Scotland? Do they get their religion at the football match? Is this the same at every match? I could not see any priests at your match in Edinburgh last week."

Tony shook his head in annoyance. He was explaining things badly. "No, you've got the wrong end of the stick again Simon."

Simon glanced around the car. "No I do not think so Mr Tony. I do not have a stick."

Tony laughed. "It's just a saying Simon. Sometimes I forget that you don't know a lot of our sayings. OK, let me see if I can make a better job of explaining this. Basically the Celtic fans tend to be Catholics and the Rangers fans are Protestants and so they tend not to like each other much. In fact they hate each other, especially on match days."

He nodded to himself. That was better. Much clearer. Simon was quiet for a moment, and he still looked a little confused. "Mr Tony, my mother she has taught me a little about these things. I always believed that both Catholics and Protestants believed in Jesus. This is not true?"

"That's right Simon, quite true."

"Then why is it that they hate each other so much when

they worship the same God? And why do they want to hate each other more when they are at a football match?"

Tony blew out his cheeks and rolled his eyes. This was ridiculous. No matter how he tried he couldn't seem to explain. "Tell you what Simon, we're nearly there now. I'll try and explain as we go along."

Simon nodded thoughtfully. He couldn't begin to work it all out. He sat quietly for a while and tried to arrange the facts in his mind. There were going to be 50,000 people at a place called Ibrox to see the Old Firm match. Some of these people were Protestant and some were Catholics which was the reason that they hated each other so much even though they worshipped the same God. They were not bad people normally. It was just that they got very excited about their religion whenever they went to a football match even though there were no priests or ceremonies or sacrifices to be seen at the match. In fact they got so excited that it was not good for little Ben to go and see this game.

He tried all he could to digest these strange facts but he could make no sense of them at all. As Tony parked the car he decided to put these matters to the back of his mind for a while.

They parked about a mile-and-a-half from the stadium and started to walk. Tony donned a thick woollen hat, put on a pair of sunglasses and pulled the collar of his coat up to his ears. Simon was surprised. Even though it was not sunny it was quite a warm day, even for him. Tony caught him looking at his sunglasses with a confused expression.

"I'd just rather not be recognised Simon. We'd keep getting stopped for autographs and we'd miss the kick off."

"What are autographs?"

Tony grinned. "Tell you later. Come on, let's stride out."

The closer they got to the ground the more Simon's eyes widened with disbelief. He had indeed thought that there had been a remarkable number of people at Easter Road the week before. But this was different. This was amazing, astonishing. There seemed to be thousands of people, millions of people. Most of them were wearing blue and red and white but quite a few were wearing green and gold and white. Everybody seemed to be singing at the top of his or her voices. This was not happy, joyous singing. This was war singing. It reminded him of the times when he was younger when he would sneak to the edge of the village at night and watch the men performing their war dances in front of the leaping flames of a huge fire.

There were policemen everywhere, many of them on horses. They seemed on edge and nervous, particularly when there were two groups of rival supporters on the same street. He noticed that Mr Tony had been absolutely right and that there were no priests to be seen anywhere.

As they walked around the corner and the stadium came into view Simon stopped and gazed at it in open amazement. Tony stopped and smiled at the look on the boy's face.

"Is this really a football ground Mr Tony?"

"It certainly is. Impressive isn't it."

The boy spoke with awe. "It is magnificent. I never believed that any building could be so big."

Once inside they bought hot-dogs and cokes and were in their seats fifteen minutes before kick-off. The noise seemed to build up with every minute that went by. Tony had taken off his shades and many of the fans around and about them were starting to recognise him. They leant over to shake his hand or clap him on the back. Programmes were passed along for him to sign and he leant across to Simon and explained "This is what we call an autograph". Simon nodded. At least one thing was clear.

All the fans that spoke to Tony had to shout to make themselves heard above the incredible noise inside the stadium. Simon could only catch snatches of what they were saying, but he kept hearing the name Jimmy Stamp. When Tony had at last finished signing programmes and scraps of paper Simon leant across and shouted in his ear. "Mr Tony, who is this Jimmy Stamp?"

For a moment Tony looked rather embarrassed. "He's a footballer. He plays for England. He and I had a bit of a run in when Scotland played England last September."

"What happened Mr Tony?"

"I hit him and broke his nose."

Simon was aghast. "What are all these men saying to you about this thing Mr Tony?"

"They say that I should hit him again when we play them in June."

Before Simon could say anything else the noise reached new and impossible levels as the two teams ran onto the pitch. Simon felt goose-bumps on his skin. The noise and the passion and the atmosphere was beyond anything he had ever imagined. The excitement was so thick in the air that he felt like he could cut it with a knife.

At last the two teams kicked off. For the first ten minutes men in green and blue shirts flew into each other as if possessed. Every incident brought the crowd baying to its feet. The supporters all around Simon and Tony kept jumping up to sing songs at the very top of their voices. Simon concentrated hard to try and make out the words.

> *"Hello! Hello!*
> *We are the Billy Boys*
> *Hello! Hello!*
> *You'll know us by our noise*
> *We're up to our knees in Fenian blood*
> *Surrender or you'll die!*
> *We are the Bridgeton Billy Boys."*

Simon tapped Tony on the shoulder "Which one is Billy Mr Tony?"

"What?"

"Billy. Which player is Billy? These men here are all singing that they are 'The Billy Boys'. I wonder which one is Billy?"

Tony couldn't help but smile. "It's not one of the players. It's King Billy."

"This King Billy he no play football Mr Tony?"

This time Tony had to laugh. "No he doesn't.

"Why are these men here his Boys then?"

"I'll tell you later in the car. Well, I'll try to."

THE DRUMS OF HAMPDEN

The pace down on the pitch remained frantic and half-time at last arrived with the game still scoreless. Celtic scored after fifteen minutes of the second half and the green and white hordes behind one of the goals went demented. All around Simon and Tony the supporters stood up and screamed at the Celtic fans until their voices seemed to crack and the veins on their necks stood out like coils of rope.

Across the ground the Celtic fans were now in full song.

> *'In hills and farms the call to arms*
> *Was heard by one and all,*
> *And from the glens came brave young men*
> *To answer Ireland's call.*
> *'Twas long ago we faced the foe,*
> *The old brigade and me,*
> *But by my side they fought and died*
> *That Ireland might be free.'*

Simon strained his ears to try and catch the words. It was too difficult. But he liked the tune. It reminded him of some of the songs he had heard the villagers singing as they picked the coffee crop.

"Mr Tony, what is this song? I think it is a beautiful tune."

"It's called 'The Boys of the Old Brigade'."Said Tony

"Was 'The Old Brigade' a football team Mr Tony?"

Tony gritted his teeth. Here we go again he thought. "No, not a team Simon."

"But the song is about football?"

"No Simon. It's about the IRA men who fought the British in 1916. It's remembering the ones who were hanged."

Again Simon's eyes widened. "This happened in Glasgow? They still hang people here I never thought these things happened in Britain Mr Tony."

"No it wasn't in Glasgow Simon. It was in Ireland. It was years and years ago and I'll try and explain it all in the car."

Simon nodded but he hadn't a clue what Tony was talking about. He had no idea that football could be so complicated.

Rangers responded to the goal like a wounded buffalo and started to pour wave after wave of attacks down on the Celtic goal. Their pressure became like an unstoppable flood and at last with only six minutes remaining on the clock they rammed home an equaliser. All around there was a mayhem of celebration. For the last few minutes the game swung wildly from end to end but neither team could score again.

Finally the referee blew his whistle and the noise and the passion started to ebb away. Honours were even. Everybody's pride remained in tact. Once again Tony disguised himself and they made their way back to the car. Once inside Simon immediately resumed his questioning.

"Mr Tony. Tell me about this King Billy. Is it right that for you here in Scotland a King is like a chief?"

"Yes Simon, that's right."

"Is King Billy a bigger chief than the Great Chief of the Clyde?"

Tony smiled. "It's not easy to say really Simon. You see King Billy ruled over two hundred years ago."

Now the boy really was amazed. "200 years ago and still these people sing his name. He must have been the greatest Chief Scotland ever had."

Tony looked a little awkward. "Well he wasn't actually. He was the king of England. In fact he originally came from Holland. He was actually called William of Orange."

"This was because his Kingdom had many oranges in it?"

"No. Orange is the name of the region where he came from in Holland."

"So he was a chief from Holland who became the King of England?"

Tony nodded. The boy continued. "Have there never been any great Chiefs here in Scotland Mr Tony? Is that why these people still want to be the 'Billy Boys'?"

"Oh we have had great kings in Scotland. The one who was probably the greatest of them all was called Robert the Bruce. He beat the English at the battle of Bannockburn and threw them out of Scotland."

"But these people do not sing about him. They do not want to be his boys?"

"No. No they don't"

Simon frowned. "Why?"

Why indeed thought Tony. "Well, they just don't Simon."

"So what was it that this King Billy did that makes all these people remember him so well?"

Tony groaned to himself silently. "OK. I'll see if I can explain it. 200 years ago there were great problems between the Protestants and the Catholics all over Europe. A King called James the Second tried to take the throne of England but he was a Catholic and so most of the people did not want him. Instead they gave the crown to a Dutch King, William of Orange – King Billy. He defeated James on the battlefield and James fled to Ireland. Most of the Irish were Catholics and they hated being ruled by the Protestant English and so they were happy when James led them in a rebellion. William went over to Ireland and defeated the Catholics at the Battle of the Boyne. He then decided that he needed more Protestants in Ireland to make sure there were no more rebellions.

"With this in mind he chose many Protestants from here in Scotland and gave them land in the north of Ireland. Of course he took this land from the Catholics who were living there. They have never forgotten this and they have been fighting for hundreds of years to get their land back. And the Protestants have been fighting for hundreds of years to keep the land that they were given."

"But Mr Tony. None of these things happened here in Scotland. King Billy was from Holland. He was made king of England and he fought battles in Ireland. I still do not understand."

Tony wasn't surprised. "Right. Of course not. Now, let me see if I can make it clearer. Over the years there were many, many bad times in Ireland. They had times when there was nothing to eat and thousands of people starved to death. When it got really bad many were forced to leave Ireland and find somewhere else to live. Many thousands went to

America. But many also came here, to Glasgow. They have never forgiven the Protestants for the land that they stole. And so this is why these people hate each other. The Irish started their own football team 100 years ago and called it Celtic. Their colours are green, white and gold – the colour of the Irish Flag and they are a magnet to the Catholics. Rangers play in blue, red and white – the colours of the Union Jack - the colours of the British flag and they became a magnet for the Protestants.

"I know that all of this must seem so crazy to you Simon and that there is no way for you to understand it. I'm sure the teachers at school will explain it better than me."

The boy gave a rather sad smile. "But you are wrong Mr Tony. You forget where I am from."

"What do you mean?"

"Mr Tony, I come from Africa. In Africa we know all about Tribalism. It is the same everywhere. Only with us it is worse. Over the mountains where you and Little Ben saw the gorillas there is Rwanda. Many years ago people from Belgium came to this place and took all the land for themselves. So that they could stay in power they gave land to one tribe and took it away from another. Just like King Billy. These tribes have hated each other for many, many years. A few years ago they started fighting. You may have seen these things on the television here Mr Tony. Many people they die. More than a million people they die. It is only the same thing. Where there are tribes there is always hate. As an African I know these things. I understand these things. I am sad to hear that it is the same here."

Simon sat back thoughtful and quiet. Tony really wanted to tell him that it was different, that it wasn't as bad as that. But in his heart he couldn't. For years his father had railed against the Sectarianism in the city and had said that it was only the same as racism. He thought of all the miserable years that the boy had endured in Mapote when he and his mother had been cut out from the life of the village. All because of colour and religion and superstition. And we look at the Africans and call them uncivilised thought Tony. How ridiculous. Simon was so very right. We are all just the same. They were both quiet on the journey home.

Simon started training the following week. Almost immediately all the other players were excited. The things he was able to do with the ball took their breath away. Tony spent the first two evenings watching quietly on the touchline. He was pleased to see how easily the young African got along with the young Glaswegians.

Tony played in the next three league games and Partick strung together two wins and a draw to move up to seventh in the table. Simon trained at Queens Park on Tuesday and Thursday evenings.

John Craig thought long and hard about when to give the boy his debut. The more he watched the boy in training the more he realised that the boy was special. Unbelievably special. He decided to wait a while. One night after Simon had been going along for three weeks Craig had a word with Tony.

"I don't know what to do mate. Part of me thinks I should keep the lad in cotton wool for a while whilst we work on his game. The other part says the hell with it and stick him in the team. The other lads are making my life a misery. Nag. Nag. Nag. Stick him in boss. Let's face it, we could use the points."

On this Craig was correct. The Queens team was one of the youngest that they had ever fielded with an average age of 21. The players were full of ability and enthusiasm but they had been finding it hard against the battle hardened pros who were winding up their careers with many of the other clubs. As the two men spoke on that cold, rainy night in March, Queens Park was second bottom of Division Three.

Tony thought for a while then said. "What exactly is it that you are worried about John?"

"Ah, you know well enough Tony. There are some hard men out there. You know how it is. Once they see just how good Simon is you know what will happen. You've been around long enough. I just want to be absolutely sure that he's ready."

"I'm not really sure you should be asking me John. I'm too close to this. There is one thing though. You have no idea how hard this lad has had it. I mean really hard. You can take the toughest estate in Glasgow and times it by three. We played in a game together when I was out there at Christmas. That's when I first saw him. There were some pretty tasty lads on the pitch and they kicked him all ends up. It all just bounced off him. Don't be fooled by his slight build. He's tough as old boots."

Craig nodded. "So give him a run then?"

"Tell you what," Said Tony "start him from the bench. Let the heat go out of the game a bit and bring him on for the second half. Most of the hard boys will be blowing a bit by then."

"OK. Sounds a good plan to me. We're up at Dumbarton on Saturday. I'll give him a go."

Craig noticed a frown on Tony's face. "What's up? Is that a problem?"

Tony shook his head. "No. No, of course not. I'm just being daft. We're away at St Johnstone, that's all. I just wish that I could be there to see it. Not to worry. Dad and Ben will go along."

The following Saturday was a typical grey Scottish winter day. A fierce wind was blowing in off the Irish Sea bringing sheet after sheet of driving, stinging rain. Dumbarton were having a mediocre season and were fifth in the division. The weather and the comparative lack of success of the home side meant that a mere 454 spectators turned up for the game. Little did any of them know that it would be a story that they would come to tell their grandchildren.

Queens Park started quite brightly and their travelling contingent of 33 fans was encouraged. However their attractive football brought nothing in the way of goals. After 23 minutes Dumbarton won a corner and their big centre half rose above everyone to head the ball home. Twelve minutes later after a wild scramble in the goalmouth they made it two.

The half-time whistle brought relief. The young Queens Park side looked down in the mouth and bedraggled as they trudged off the field. However once in the dressing-room their mood soon lifted.

"Alright you lot, you've all been making my life a misery over the last couple of weeks and to be honest I've had enough. So you can have it your way. I'm sticking Simon on for the second half."

There was an immediate straightening of backs. "You've all seen what he can do. Now it's time to let him loose. Now I presume you all know what the Number 10 position is. The Number 10 plays between the front two and the midfield. He plays in the hole. The centre halfs don't know if they should pick him up and the centre midfield doesn't know whether to leave their men and drop back. OK?"

There were eager nods.

"Good. So Simon is our Number 10. He has a free role. He can just float. All you lot have to do is get him the ball." Craig nodded to Charlie Nish. Nish was the oldest player in the team. He had been a stalwart of the Queens Park midfield for over ten years whilst working as a builder through the week. He was heavily muscled and had a face like a piece of granite. "Charlie, you mind him out there OK? Anyone who wants to play the hard man has to deal with you. Let them know. You know the score."

Nish grinned. It wasn't a pretty sight. When he spoke his voice was like an angle grinder. He walloped Simon on the back and nearly knocked him off the bench. "You're alright with me lad. You just get out there and do your stuff. I'll watch your back."

Five minutes into the second half Simon picked up a pass ten yards into the Dumbarton half. He skipped over a lunging challenge and bore down on the goal. The first centre half moved out and threw himself into a wild two-footed tackle. Simon slipped the ball by him and jumped the tackle as easily as a gazelle leaping over a log. He dropped his left shoulder and glided past the last defender before clipping a deft chip over the keeper and into the top corner of the goal.

For a moment there was a stunned silence around the ground. Even the 33 travelling fans seemed too stunned to cheer. Then they leapt around in glee whilst the Dumbarton fans shook their heads in amazement. By the time the final whistle was blown Simon had completed his hat-trick and laid on two more goals. Dumbarton had themselves scored twice. Nish had been yellow-carded for almost breaking an over-eager home midfielder into two pieces. Dumbarton 4 – Queens Park 5. A legend was born. None of those present at the tiny Scottish stadium would ever forget seeing the great Simon Matembo make his debut.

Tony ran off the pitch following Partick's 1 – 1 draw in Perth and ripped his radio out of his bag. He sat feeling frustrated as reporters from grounds all over Scotland summed up their games. Then at last he heard what he was waiting for. There had been no reporter present at Dumbarton that afternoon and so it was the studio presenter who gave out the news.

" . . . and finally I must give you news of a remarkable game at Dumbarton. The home side were leading comfortably 2 – 0 at half-time. Then Queens Park gave a debut to seventeen-year-old Simon Matembo who came on from the bench. Matembo scored a second half hat-trick and made two as Queens Park went on to win 5 – 4. Sounds like some kind of a game. Young Matembo is clearly a man to watch out for . . ."

Tony punched the air and shouted "YES!!!". His team-mates looked over with interest.

"Never knew you were such a Queens Park fan skip."

Tony's grin spit his face in two. "Course I am. Always have been."

He met up with Ben and Winston and Simon in a McDonalds on the edge of the city an hour later. Within a few minutes Simon was half-way through his third Big Mac. After a lifetime of maize cakes and yams the boy have developed a total passion for *Big Macs*. When he completed his third burger he gave Tony a hopeful look.

"You're going look like a Big Mac if you keep eating them at this rate Simon." Tony rolled his eyes and then passed over a two-pound coin. "Go on, you've earned it."

Soon many of the kids in the restaurant recognised him and came over for autographs. Tony smiled as he signed them. He looked over to Simon. "I better enjoy this while it lasts. I don't think it will be long before they won't be bothered about my autograph. You, my boy, are going to be a star."

When Ben and Simon went up to the counter to order ice-cream Tony spoke to his father.

"So Dad. How was he?"

Winston had been unusually quiet. "He was amazing. Absolutely amazing. Don't get me wrong Tony. I knew he was good. But what I saw today was not like anything I have ever seen before. We are going to have to look after this boy very carefully Tony. Remember the promises we have made to his Mummy. School first. It is not going to be easy."

Tony grinned. "Well it's lucky he's got a good agent. If anyone can scare the press to death it's you Dad."

The following Wednesday night Tony led the Scotland side out to meet Latvia at Hampden Park. It was an absolutely must win game for Scotland. Nothing but three points would do. It soon turned into a classic match. Both of the teams were well matched as the ball fizzed around the pitch in quick passing moves. The Latvians took the lead in the 29th minute but Scotland were back on level terms before half-time. Tony revelled in the speed of the game and found once again that his passing was at its best.

The second half was a feast of open attacking football. Both goalkeepers performed heroics on many occasions. Scotland at last scored their winning goal in the 78th minute.

As the players celebrated in the dressing room they heard the news from Anfield where England had been playing Italy. The Italians had nicked the points with a winning goal in the 85th minute and the qualifying group was suddenly wide open.

NEW RECRUIT

Team	P	W	L	D	Points
England	6	4	1	1	13
Scotland	6	3	1	2	11
Italy	5	3	1	1	10
Latvia	6	2	4	0	6
Luxemb'g	6	0	6	0	0

Two games to go. And what games! In May Scotland would travel to play the mighty Italians in Rome's Olympic Stadium. It had been years since anyone had got a result there. But the English had beaten the Italians in Milan. So it was possible. Very, very hard . . . but possible. And if they managed a win then they would have a chance of stealing second place in the group by beating the English at Hampden in the final game in June.

Tony sat drinking a can of lager and thought that one more win would bring on his rematch with Jimmy Stamp. A rematch at Hampden! He felt fit and in the form of his life. It couldn't come quickly enough.

But first they would have to deal with Italy.

Chapter 11
Rome

March and the first half of April seemed to go by in a blur. Amazing things were afoot at Hampden Park. In the week following the 5 – 4 thriller at Dumbarton whispers about Simon Matembo drifted around the city like a breeze. In pubs and cafes and workshops and school yards there was a buzz of conversation. Who was this boy? Where had he come from? How good was he? Could he really be as good as they said he was?

Word soon leaked out that the boy had come to Scotland with Tony Hobbes and was staying with the Scottish captain and his family. The doorbell kept ringing as expectant journalists hoped to get a glimpse of the new wonder-boy.

When Simon once again made a half-time entrance to make his home debut against East Stirlingshire the following Saturday there were 3,472 spectators inside the National Stadium. It was Queen's Park's highest home crowd for years. This time Simon scored twice as the home side won 2 – 1. The second goal had the crowd on their feet. The Queens keeper punted a long kick down field. Simon leapt up and took the ball on his chest. As the ball dropped he clipped it over is shoulder and spun past his marker. He met the dropping ball on the volley and hit it into the net like a tracer-bullet. From the keeper's hands to the back of the net the ball had never touched the ground.

This time the press box was more than half-full and the next day the papers were filled with buoyant reports from usually hard-nosed, cynical journalists. Two of them mentioned the name Pele in their pieces.

THE DRUMS OF HAMPDEN

The following week Queens Park travelled up to Elgin City. The tiny ground was quite incapable of accommodating all the fans that wanted to get in. The gates were closed an hour before the kick off. The game finished 3 – 3. Simon again scored twice. The legend continued to grow.

Queens Park's next home game was in the middle of April. For the visit of Ross County an amazing 23,483 half-filled the Stadium. They were a mixed assortment. Many were dyed in the wool football enthusiasts who had travelled from all over Britain to see the new, young star in the flesh. Many were youngsters who flocked to see the boy with the magic in his feet. And of course many were scouts drawn like bees to the honey pot from clubs the length and breadth of Europe. This time Simon only scored once – a weaving, jinking run that took him past six desperate challenges before he softly lifted the ball over the diving keeper.

The media laid siege in their anxiety for an interview. Winston strode out and stone walled their pleading. No, there wouldn't be any interviews today. No there weren't any plans for any interviews. He angrily waved his arms to make the reporters quieten down.

"Now listen and listen good! Let us get some facts straight right here and now. This boy is an amateur. He is seventeen years old and his first priority is school. Like many young men before him he is playing for this great amateur club in his spare time. He receives no wages and therefore is under no obligation to talk to any of you. Now please, leave him alone!"

With this Winston stormed from the room but he was becoming anxious. Later he sat down with his son. "Tony, this is getting difficult. All the media are desperate for this story. I think you and I had better call a press conference. Let's tell them a little about how you came to meet Simon and where he is from. I feel we have to give them something. We can emphasise the reason why there are to be no interviews. Hopefully it might make them back off a little."

"OK Dad, you know best."

ROME

The following Tuesday afternoon Tony received a call from Bill Duncan, the Scotland manager. "Hi Tony, are you busy this afternoon?"

"No Bill, not particularly."

"Could you pop down to Hampden for a wee chat?"

"Sure. Where and when?"

"Sir Robert's office. Say in an hour?"

"Fine."

As Tony drove across the city he wondered what on earth the meeting was all about. The following Saturday Scotland was due to meet the Italians in Rome. They were scheduled to fly out on Thursday. Maybe it was something to do with the game.

As Tony walked into Sir Robert's office he was met with two very anxious looking men. Sir Robert smiled briefly and waived Tony to a seat.

"Tony, thanks for coming at such short notice. It's appreciated. Bill, would you like to fill Tony in?"

Duncan nodded. "Sure. Hobbo, we've got a nightmare on our hands. I've been getting calls from managers all day yesterday and all morning today. It's a disaster. We've got an injury crisis the likes of which I've never seen. It's unbelievable. I've lost four strikers, two midfielders and three defenders. It's catastrophe."

Tony sat back in his chair and groaned. Why did it have to be now? Of all the games and it had to be now. He felt as if he had been punched in the stomach. "Go on then boss. Who's out?"

They ran through the names for a few minutes and tried to look at different options and systems. Whichever way they looked at it the picture looked black. If a draw had been of any use at all them maybe they could have come up with something. But a draw was of no use whatsoever. Only a win would do. And a win would be hard enough to achieve in Rome even with a full squad. Now that they were down to the bare bones it seemed almost impossible. The three men sat quietly for a while staring down at Duncan's scribbled diagrams. At last Sir Robert cleared his throat and spoke.

"There is maybe one option Tony."

"Well fire away Sir Robert. We need something. Anything."

"Your lad. Simon. Simon Matembo. I watched him last week. He's special. I know it is a heck of a long shot, but what is his passport situation?"

Tony was stunned for a moment. He hadn't even begun to see this coming. Of course! It was so obvious. That was why they had wanted him to come down to Hampden.

He spoke quietly. "The passport isn't a problem. Simon has a British passport. His dad was Scottish."

"Good Lord." Said Sir Robert. The two men stared at Tony. The silence stretched and stretched. At last Tony felt that he had to break it. "You got me down here because you want to take Simon to Rome, correct?"

Duncan nodded. Tony continued. "This puts me in a difficult situation. I promised his mum that Simon would concentrate of his education before everything else when he came here. I wanted him to keep a low profile for a couple of years until he finished his studies . . ."

Tony let the sentence die. Sir Robert carefully lit his pipe and then spoke. "I don't think that a low profile is much of an option any more Tony. The cat is well and truly out of the bag now. It doesn't matter that Simon is only playing for Queens Park, he is like a magnet. The only chance of a low profile is if the boy doesn't play at all, and I very much doubt if that would be what he would want."

"No." Said Tony "You're right there. It would kill him not to play. He lives and breathes football."

Again there was a silence. Tony knew that the decision that he had to make was a hugely important one. If he allowed Simon to travel to Rome then the media frenzy would only get worse. He agonised over all the promises that he had made to Rose whilst sitting outside her hut in far away Mapote. One the other hand Sir Robert was right. The media was not going to go away now that they had seen what Simon could do. Sure, the boy was only seventeen. But Tony had only been nineteen when he had won his first cap. At last he breathed out slowly.

"OK he can come to Rome, but only on my terms. Just like John Craig is doing at Queens Park, he sits on the bench. When we get into the second half I will give the signal for him to come on, but on one condition. He can only come on if there is a chance that he can make a difference. If we are getting hammered, he stays on the bench. Likewise, if we are winning by a street, he stays on the bench. If you'll agree to these terms then he can get on the plane."

Both men nodded emphatically. The deal was done. Tony drove straight to Simon's school and arrived just in time to meet him at the gates. "Hang on a sec, Simon. I'm just going to park up. We need to pop in and see the headmaster."

"Mr Tony, I hope that there isn't a problem." The desperate look of seriousness on the boy's face made Tony chuckle.

"No problem whatsoever."

"Then what is it?"

"Wait and see."

They made their way to the head's office and knocked on the door. "Come in!"

The Head broke into a wide smile as soon as he saw Tony. With Simon's magical talent and Tony's Thursday night coaching sessions Highfield were taking the Glasgow football world by storm.

"Mr Hobbes. Wonderful to see you. Please, take a seat. What can I do for you?"

"Well I'm afraid I'm the bearer of good and bad news. The bad news is that Simon will have to take a couple of days off at the end of the week and so I'm afraid he will miss your semi-final match."

The Head's face fell. This was indeed a crushing blow. Just when they were so close to reaching the final for the first time in their history. He couldn't imagine what good news could possibly soften such a terrible blow. Tony carried on.

"The good news is the reason. Simon has been selected for the Scotland squad to play Italy on Saturday. It isn't every school has one of its pupils play for his country whilst still an amateur."

Simon and the Headmaster both looked as if they had been smacked in the face with a wet towel The Head recovered first. "This is . . . well it's . . . I mean it's . . . it's just marvellous. Absolutely marvellous. Well done young man. Wonderful."

Simon was staring at Tony with eyes the size of saucers. "Is it really true Mr Tony?"

"Yes Simon. It is. Absolutely true."

"So this time we can play together. I have hoped very much for this day. I have longed to play with you another time Mr Tony." As Tony realised that the boy was far more overjoyed by the fact that they would be playing for the same team than the fact that he had been picked to play for Scotland he felt his eyes well with tears. He choked slightly. "Me too Simon. Me too."

He turned back to the headmaster who seemed to have grown about two feet. "I need to ask a small favour. We want to keep Simon's inclusion in the squad as low key as possible. He will fly out from Manchester with my Dad tomorrow morning. All a bit cloak-and-dagger I'm afraid. We would rather the press didn't get wind of it, or the Italians for that matter. Let's leave it as a big surprise to be announced an hour before the game."

The Head nodded. Part of him was itching to tell everybody that he knew. But being part of the secret appealed as well. He nodded firmly. "Of course Mr Hobbes. My lips are sealed." He smiled at Simon. "And you young man, well, you just knock them dead."

It was like walking out into a sea of noise as Tony led the team out onto the Olympic Stadium pitch the following Saturday. Flags. Flares. Smoke. Horns. Sheer Latin passion. Everyone had kept the secret. The first that anyone realised about Simon's inclusion in the squad was when the team was announced an hour before the game. Tony sensed a buzz of anticipation amongst the 10,000 travelling Scotland fans as they watched Simon warm up in his tracksuit.

In the first half things went better than he could have hoped. Italy of course enjoyed long periods of possession but they were naturally cautious. Even though the Scotland side was seriously weakened they were reluctant to commit everything to attack. The crowd, which had started by baying for Scottish blood, soon became quieter and quieter and more and more frustrated. Once again Tony felt in the form of his life. He now realised that the long enforced break was the best thing that could have happened to him. For year after year he had been playing with niggling injuries. He had hardly ever been 100 percent fit. The long lay-off had given his body a rest that it had desperately needed.

Now he felt fitter than he did as a teenager. His legs seemed to eat up the turf and he was filled with a confidence that he had never known. Time and again in that first half he positioned himself perfectly to break up Italian attacks. He never mistimed a tackle. He never committed a foul.

When the referee blew for half-time Tony was delighted with the team's performance. His only concern was that Scotland had failed to create a single clear-cut chance. The mighty Italian defence had brushed every effort aside.

Things soon changed in the second half. The Italy manager had really got his team fired-up. They started to hammer away at Scotland and the pressure grew steadily. The crowd sensed their team's change in mood and the noise grew and grew. Tony could feel the tension and the strain in his fellow players, many of whom had little or no international experience. It seemed as if the crowd was a twelfth player for Italy. The men in Azzuri blue seemed to suck in energy and passion from the vast Roman masses. Their passes got quicker and quicker. The ball was now fizzing over the turf in a blur. At times the speed of their feet and the level of their skills was breathtaking. Tony put every ounce of energy he had into marshalling the defence. Somehow the Scots held the line, but with every minute that went by it was getting harder. Then at last the damn broke. In the 68th minute they finally broke through as their centre half headed home from a corner.

Tony tried to lift the players but it was difficult. The younger players were tiring and the Italian defenders were finding it easier and easier to break down the Scottish attacks.

Play was halted whilst a player received treatment. Tony glanced over to the touchline where Simon was energetically running up and down. Bill Duncan was standing out of the dugout and giving him a pleading look.

It was time.

They needed Simon. Tony nodded to Duncan and he quickly waved Simon over to tell him to get ready. He came on three minutes later to wild cheers from the Scotland fans.

There were still fifteen minutes of the game left.

Tony managed to slip the ball to him a couple of minutes later. The stadium held its breath as he slipped past the two central defenders and chipped the keeper. The ball seemed to hang in the air for an eternity before dropping onto the crossbar. The Italy keeper dived on the ball gratefully.

Simon's break scared the Italians to death. Their frantic manager shouted instructions and immediately two men moved over to mark Simon. Italy did all they could to waste time and to keep possession. Tony felt a rising panic as Scotland chased and chased to try and get the ball.

The clock was ticking down. There were only minutes to go. At last he made a big tackle in the centre of the field. He sensed Simon spin and break fast down the right wing. He flipped the ball forward and cursed himself. It was too high!

As he ran forward he saw Simon jump high with his back arched. Somehow he seemed to twist in the air and take the ball on his chest. As he was dropping he clipped the ball over the last defender. He hit the ground and he was away.

Tony drove himself forward with every ounce of energy that he had left in his body. The last defender pounded across and slid into a tackle on the African. He had no intention of winning the ball. He was looking to deposit Simon in the second row of the stand. Simon managed to jump the instant before the tackle hit him full on. Still the defender caught his leg and he landed awkwardly. For a moment it seemed that he couldn't possibly keep his footing. For three strides it looked a certainty that he would fall. Then he at last regained his balance and caught the ball just before it crossed the goal line.

Tony was arriving in the penalty area at full speed. Simon's cross, whipped over. It was too far. Too far! Tony didn't think that he could make it. His lungs were on fire. He threw himself into a dive. He stretched his neck. He stretched every part of his body and the ball hit his forehead with a meaty thump. A split second before he hit the ground he saw the ball flying toward the top corner like a bullet.

As he crashed to the ground the stadium seemed to explode. The massed ranks of the Scottish fans were behind the goal where Tony had scored. They went absolutely berserk. As he picked himself up off the floor he saw Simon jogging back from the touchline giving the supporters a shy wave. Then they were both mobbed by their team-mates.

Tony had to shake them off and shout. "Right. That's enough. Pack it in. We're not there yet. We DON'T want a draw. Only a win will do! So come on! Concentrate. Get tight."

As he watched them restart the game Tony could see that the Italy team had been hit hard by the goal. They were vulnerable. Nervous. Simon's skill had scared them half to death. For five minutes the game was bogged down in the centre of the park as both sets of players flew at each other.

Tony received a short pass and was looking for Simon when he found himself in mid-air. The Italian centre forward had crashed into him from behind. As he hit the ground in a heap he heard the whistle blow and the Scottish end of the ground resounded with boos. There could only be seconds to go.

He grabbed the ball and heaved himself quickly to his feet. Simon was ten yards away. He gave him the ball. The Italy team was taken by surprise by the speed of the free kick.

Simon turned as he took the ball. He started to run for goal. Tony's chest was pounding and his legs felt like lead weights. The foul had taken all the wind from him. He could do no more than stand and watch.

The scene that he watched unfold was absolutely breathtaking. Simon glided past four wild tackles and rounded the keeper before rolling the ball slowly into the net.

Within seconds his slim frame was completely submerged by the white shirts of his team-mates. He heard the referee blow his whistle three times. Full-time. It was over. They had done it.

Tony sank down to the ground and fought to catch his breath. The ground rocked with the noise of the Scotland supporters. The other players had lifted Simon to their shoulders and they were taking the acclaim of the fans.

Giuseppe Fiore, the Italian centre-half and captain, walked slowly over to where Tony was sitting and held out a hand. Tony took it and the Italian heaved him to his feet. They had played in the Liverpool team years before and had shared a room for away games.

"You make a great game Tony."

"Thanks Giuseppe. You too." He was still so short of breath that he could hardly speak.

Fiore shook his head as both men watched the Scotland players bounce Simon up and down on their shoulders.

"I've never seen anything like him Tony. Never."

"Neither have I. He's special."

"Well I hope he does the same to England, Si?"

Tony grinned. "Si."

When he was at last put down onto the floor Simon trotted over to where Tony still waited on the half way line. "Are you OK Mr Tony?"

Tony had to laugh when he saw the look of serious concern on Simon's face. "Of course I am. Just a bit winded, that's all. Otherwise I've never felt better in my life. Come on; let's get you back to the dressing room. No reporters, OK?"

"OK Mr Tony. It was a very great header."

"It was a very great cross."

They both laughed as they left the pitch. The dressing room was a place of celebration. It soon got a whole lot better. News came in from St James's Park that England had been held to a 0-0 draw by the Latvians. All of a sudden the group had been thrown wide open.

Team	P	W	L	D	Points
England	7	4	1	2	14
Scotland	7	4	1	2	14
Italy	6	3	2	1	10
Latvia	7	2	4	1	7
Luxemb'g	7	0	7	0	0

The dressing room was soon under siege from reporters demanding to interview Simon. Tony took a long swig of water and went out to handle them. The first interview was with Andy Gray of *Sky TV* who had screened the match live.

He talked to Tony as they set up the microphone.

"Come on Hobbo. Surely you'll give us a quick word with the new lad."

"No Andy. No interviews. Not yet. Give the lad a break. He's only a kid."

Gray was desperate. "Give me a break will you! The whole world will want to hear him after what he just did. I've never seen anything like it! Please Hobbo, name your price."

Tony chuckled. "Calm down Andy. The world is just going to have to be patient and só are you. The answer is no and there is no price. You'll just have to make do with me."

A deep, loud voice spoke from behind them. It was Winston. "Is this Tele man givin' you trouble Tony?"

Gray groaned. "Hello Winston."

"Hello Andy. This boy is not ready for any TV yet. When he is ready I will tell you. Now you talk to Tony."

Tony worked his way through several interviews and it was 40 minutes before he was able to get back to the dressing-room to shower and change. When they left the ground to get on the coach there were hundreds of Scottish fans waiting to cheer them.

That night pictures of the Scotland win were beamed to just about every country on earth. The game that united the planet from Chile to Japan and from Mexico to South Africa had found a new hero. A star had been born in the noise and the passion of Rome's footballing Coliseum.

Tony sat alone at the front of the coach as it made its way to the airport. He enjoyed the quiet and the sense of triumph. He was delighted when he glanced back up the bus to see Simon laughing and joking with a group of the younger players. What a day! Five young players had pulled on Scotland shirts for the first time and they had broken through the mighty Italy defence and had taken the national team within touching distance of the Euro 2004 finals. One more game to go. And what a game! Football's oldest and most deadly rivals would face each other at Hampden in June; Tony felt a smile spread slowly across his face. He had promised Jimmy Stamp that the next time it would be different. It seemed like a lifetime had passed since he had met with Stamp at his London home when Tony's career had come to its lowest ebb.

So much had changed since then. Africa. The gorillas. The game in Misumba. And Simon. The boy with the magic in his feet. Tony pictured Stamp's leering, cocky face. Well this time it would be different. Jimmy Stamp didn't know what was going to hit him.

In its long and proud history Hampden Park had seen some mighty encounters. But the game in June promised to be the mightiest of them all.

Chapter 12
Disaster Strikes

Tony awoke the next morning in a fantastic mood. The flight hadn't landed in Glasgow until 2.00 a.m. and it had been well after three by the time they had got to bed. He had only had a few hours sleep but he didn't feel remotely tired. The warm afterglow of their magnificent night in Rome still filled his body. The April sun was shining strongly through the bedroom window and all seemed well with his world. He pulled on his dressing-gown and looked out. A knot of reporters was camped out on the pavement outside the house. It wasn't much of a surprise. They could wait there all week as far as he was concerned.

He went downstairs and switched on the kettle. He pulled a £10 note from his wallet and went into the lounge where Ben and Simon were watching the television.

"Morning lads. Lovely morning. Ben, take this tenner and pop down to the newsagent and buy a copy of every Sunday paper that you can find. I'm afraid that you better not go with him Simon, there's a gang of reporters outside . . ."

His voice trailed off as he noticed their faces. Ben looked pale and worried. Tears were running down Simon's cheeks. Tony was aghast. "Good Lord. What on earth has happened?"

Ben pointed to the TV screen. "Look Dad. It's terrible. There's been a volcano in Uganda. It is near Mapote."

Simon spoke very softly. "It is a mountain in the Ruwenzori. We call it Batumba, 'The Evil One'. It is many years since it has exploded. Old men tell of how things are when Batumba is angry. When Batumba is angry things are very bad in Mapote."

Tony sat down slowly and watched the pictures on the screen with horror. A huge pillar of smoke and dust had climbed high into the sky from the volcano. The reporter was speaking into his microphone under the shelter of a veranda. He explained that millions of tonnes of volcanic dust were falling across a huge area of eastern Uganda. As well as the dust there had been rocks thrown from the volcano like artillery shells. Some of these rocks were the size of cars and many casualties were reported.

The whole area had been plunged into chaos and the emergency services were quite unable to cope. The hospital at Kabale was already full to overflowing.

The report finished with several shots which showed how the beautiful rolling green hills were now coated in a choking layer of volcanic ash.

Simon spoke in a small voice. "Mr Tony. I must go back. I must find out if my mother is OK. I cannot stay here."

Tony nodded. "Of course you must. But let me think."

He made his coffee and forced himself to think clearly. He remembered the small, pot-holed roads that lead from Kampala to Mapote. It was a two-day drive even in the best of times. How long would it take now? By the time that they got a flight and found a car . . . it would take at least a week. He stopped himself as he realised that he was thinking in terms of "we". Well of course he was. There was no way that he would allow Simon to return alone, no way at all.

He considered the complications and remembered with relief that there was no football for a fortnight. The following weekend was clear. Even so, the club would not be happy at him going off to the disaster area in Uganda. He brushed the thought aside. The club would have to lump it.

He racked his brain. There was no way that he could allow Simon to have to wait a whole week for news of his mother. The tension would be awful for the boy. But what else could he do? There were very few phones in the Mapote district and he felt that what ones there were would almost certainly be damaged. Then an idea hit him.

He grabbed the phone and started to make calls. It took him five calls before he had the information that he needed – Andy Gray's home number.

He dialed and drummed his fingers impatiently as he waited for an answer. Gray's unmistakable Scottish voice came on the line. "Hello."

"Andy. It's Tony Hobbes speaking."

Surprised. "Oh, morning Hobbo, what can I do for you?"

"Yesterday you asked me to name a price for you to get an interview with Simon. I have a price."

"Go on."

"Have you seen the news?"

Gray sounded confused. "Well, yes and no. I've had the radio on. I haven't really listened though."

"Have you heard about the volcano in Uganda."

"Yes, I heard something."

Tony took a deep breath. "Good. Now listen. Simon comes from a village that is right in the middle of the disaster area. His mother is there and the poor lad is worried sick. He wants to go straight back but there is no way that we will be able to get there for days. Now *Sky* have a news team in the area. I've just watched their report. If you can get them to go to Mapote and find out about his mum, we will give you an exclusive interview."

Gray sounded concerned. "This is awful Hobbo. Don't worry. I'll do what I can. Wait by the phone."

"One more thing Andy. Please don't give the story any publicity until you find out how the news is. I don't want Simon to get any bad news from the television. If the news is good and Rose is OK you will have a great story and an exclusive interview."

"Leave it with me Hobbo."

Tony went back into the lounge and told Simon about what was happening. Gray called back half an hour later and told him that *Sky* were contacting their team in Uganda and sending them to Mapote.

The day seemed to last forever as they sat and waited for the phone to ring. By four in the afternoon Tony's nerves were stretched to breaking point when the phone started to ring. He grabbed the receiver. "Hobbo, it's Andy here. It's good news. Our people made it through to the village and they found out that Rose Matembo is in her college in Kampala. The village is not too badly damaged. There weren't too many hits by the big rocks it seems. There are one or two injuries but nothing serious. The bad news is the coffee crop. It's destroyed. There will be no harvest this year."

Tony sagged with relief and immediately told Simon the wonderful news. He resumed his conversation. "I can't thank you enough for this Andy. I owe you one."

The Scot chuckled. "And you'll pay me one too."

All through the afternoon news coverage of the disaster the television had been advertising the number for a Relief Fund which had been set up to provide much needed aid to the stricken region. As Tony sat back down the number was once again on the screen. Simon said. "Mr Tony. Is there anything that we could do to help this fund? With no coffee there will be a very bad time in Mapote."

Tony sat back and thought. As he thought his gaze fell upon a picture on the wall. As he stared at the picture the germ of an idea grew in his mind. The more he stared, the more it grew. At last he leapt to his feet and clapped his hands. "Yes Simon. There is something. It is a real long-shot, but I think there is definitely something that we can do."

He quickly ran through the bones of his plan and Simon was very thoughtful. Eventually the boy spoke.

"Mr Tony, I cannot understand many of these things, but this seems a very wonderful plan that you have made. There is maybe one thing you could think of. It is the team Mr Tony. Maybe we could do something else that is good. Instead of it being a Scotland team maybe it could be a team made up from Celtic and Rangers players. Maybe this is a thing that could help them not to hate each other so much." He gave a small smile. "Well, that is if they would allow you and me to play for this team."

Tony looked hard at the boy. "You're right Simon. You're absolutely right. And don't worry, I'll make sure that we get a game. Now, let's see if I can turn this dream into reality."

He made several more calls and then left the house. He completely ignored the gaggle of reporters and jumped into his car. He drove to a hotel on the outskirts of the city and one by one several players arrived. They were mainly senior pros from both Celtic and Rangers. The bar staff looked on in amazement as the arch-rivals chatted and joked over their drinks. When they were all gathered Tony stood up and spoke to them.

"OK guys, listen up. You probably don't know, but that big volcano that has gone off in Uganda is right by the place where Simon lives. Now there is a big appeal for help and I for one am going to do something. I have something in mind. If it comes off it will mean all of us going to Uganda. Now let me tell you all about it . . ."

An hour later he left the hotel. All the players were with him. His next stop was to see the two Chairmen of Celtic and Rangers. He made more calls on his mobile phone and agreed to meet them in a city centre hotel. He also got Sir Robert Hyde to agree to attend the meeting. They talked for two hours but in the end they agreed that the players should be allowed to go. "If you can pull it off in Cape Town and get *Sky* on board you can leave all the detailed arrangements to the S.F.A." Said Sir Robert. "The last thing you will want to be worrying about is visas and hotel bookings. Best of luck Tony. You deserve it."

His last call was his father's house. He had kept his dad informed of events in Uganda all day but he hadn't told him of his plan. As he walked into the house he said to Winston. "Right dad. Upstairs and pack a bag. We need to be on the road in half an hour. I have a hotel room booked at Heathrow and if we move now we'll make it before midnight. You'll need two days off work."

Winston raised his hands to slow Tony down. "Now steady on boy and talk to me properly. What do I need a bag for? Why are we goin' to Heathrow? Where are we goin'?"

"South Africa. I've booked the tickets and we land in Cape Town tomorrow evening."

When Tony explained why his father was more than happy to take two days off work.

Chapter 13
Pay for view

Tony, Winston and Simon took the 5.00 a.m. flight from Heathrow and landed in Cape Town many hours later. They were all exhausted by the flight and they went quickly off to bed in their hotel after a quick snack. Before he turned off the lights Tony placed a call to England and spoke again to Andy Gray.

"Did you find anything out Andy?"

"Yes. You're a lucky boy Hobbo. He will be at the Residence all morning and according to his official diary there doesn't seem to be anything planned."

"Brilliant." Tony was hugely relieved. "What are the people at *Sky* saying?"

"If you can come up with the goods tomorrow they are happy to back you."

More good news. "Listen, that's fantastic Andy. Thanks for all your help."

"Don't mention it. You still owe me that interview remember."

Tony laughed. "Well I don't think you are likely to let me forget it in a hurry."

They ate breakfast early and climbed into a taxi a little after eight. The sleep had put Winston in a growly mood and he grumped and groaned for the whole journey. "This is the most stupid thing I have ever done. This man is one of the busiest men in the world. He's not goin' to find time to see two-bit people like us. You just wait and see. This is just a wild goose chase . . ."

At last the Taxi dropped them off outside a huge set of metal gates which were guarded by a police post. Two policemen stepped out to meet them as they approached the gates.

"Can we help you gentlemen?"

"Yes." Said Tony brightly. "We would like to see President Mandela."

The policeman first looked quite bemused, and then a small recognition came into his eyes. "You are Tony Hobbes. Scotland captain, yes?"

Tony beamed. "That is correct."

"Do you have an appointment?"

"No."

"Then what you ask is quite impossible Mr Hobbes."

Tony reached into his shoulder-bag and pulled out the picture from his lounge wall, which had caught his attention the afternoon before. It was a picture of himself and President Nelson Mandela. It had been taken nine years before when Liverpool had toured South Africa. The photo had been taken after a game that the club had played in the township of Soweto. The club had been reluctant to play the game due to violence in the surrounding area. Tony had persuaded the players to go ahead with the game and President Mandela had been very grateful.

"Please take this to him and tell him that I am waiting outside. I need to discuss a very urgent matter. It will only take a few minutes."

The policemen looked doubtful but he went into the command post and spoke on the telephone. A few minutes later a man in a suit came to collect the photo. A further twenty minutes passed before the man in the suit returned. He spoke quickly to the policemen and then came over to Tony.

"Mr Hobbes. Our President sends his compliments. He will see you now."

Tony turned to wink at his father as they were led along a succession of long corridors. Simon was like a mouse. As they were ushered into a fine old office Nelson Mandela rose from he desk and smiled. He was older than when Tony had last seen him but he still had a remarkable presence.

"Well Tony. What a pleasant surprise. I apologise that you were kept waiting. Please introduce me to your colleagues. In fact, wait a minute. I already know this boy. If I am not mistaken you are Simon Matembo. I think all of South Africa saw your goal at the weekend. Please sit down."

Coffee was brought and Mandela asked politely about their flight and hotel. He never mentioned the unorthodox nature of their arrival. "Now Tony, you said that you came with urgent business?"

"Indeed Mr President. You will be aware of the situation in Uganda?"

Mandela frowned. "Indeed I am. The situation is very grave."

Tony pressed on. "Well Simon comes from a village in the centre of the disaster area. A place called Mapote. He asked me if there was anything that we could do to help the Relief Appeal. Well I think that there is, but I will need your help."

Mandela was intrigued. "Continue please."

"Well." Said Tony, "I have had discussions with several of the players at Celtic and Rangers and the management of the two clubs. I have also had discussions with *Sky TV*. In a nutshell, a joint team is willing to go to Uganda to play a game to raise money for the Appeal. Of course Simon and

I would play as honorary guests. *Sky* is willing to show the game on 'Pay-for-View' all over the world and donate the proceeds to the Appeal. We have three very famous pop groups who will come out with us and perform live before the game. Everything is nearly in place. All we need now is some opposition. I think that we should play South Africa. Now that is where I need your help."

Mandela laughed aloud with delight at the idea. "Tony, is this really all your own idea?"

"Amazingly enough, yes, it is."

"Then you are to be congratulated. Of course we will field a side, hopefully a good side. Tell me, have you made arrangements yet with the Ugandan Government?"

"No. I was waiting to speak with you before talking to them."

"No problem. Please leave all of that to me. I know President Kumba well. We are old friends. All you need to do is turn up and all will be arranged. When is the game to be?"

"I'm afraid that the only time that *Sky* can fit it in is next Sunday."

Mandela whistled. "Five days. Not very long, but long enough. We shall have to be quick on our feet. The good news is that I have a free weekend and so I shall be able to come myself. I look forward to seeing more of you young man."

He smiled at Simon who was acutely embarrassed. "Thank you sir." was all that he could manage to say.

The next few days seemed to pass in a blur. Within hours of their meeting with the President, *Sky* started to put their advertising machine into overdrive. They sent Andy Gray and a news team to Kampala to meet Tony, Winston and Simon when they got off the plane from Cape Town. There were huge crowds of Ugandans at the airport to cheer their new hero. The promised interview was carried out in the garden of their hotel.

Simon and Tony sat across from Andy Gray at a small table.

" . . . tell me Tony," said Gray "was it your idea to field a joint Celtic/Rangers side?"

Tony smiled. "Actually it wasn't. My idea was to field a Scotland side. It was Simon who came up with the idea of the 'Old Firm'."

Gray turned to Simon. "Why was that Simon?"

"Mr Tony, he take me to see one of these 'Old Firm' games. It was a very exciting game and the stadium was very beautiful. But I was very sad when I saw how much these people hate each other. Mr Gray, I am an African. I have seen how much pain and suffering there can be when two tribes hate each other. Mr Tony and me met President Mandela last week. He is a very great man. He has shown all of us that tribes can make peace as well as war. I hope this game can help."

"And the shirts, Simon, were they your idea?"

"No Mr Gray. Mr Tony has made this idea."

Gray chuckled. "My goodness, I never saw you as a fashion designer. You'll be giving Scottish hard men midfielders a bad name."

"I'm not getting any younger Andy, maybe fashion is a field I should be looking at."

The shirts in question had indeed been an absolute brain wave. They were half Celtic green and white and half Rangers blue. One of the big sportswear companies had manufactured them at breakneck speed and £15 from every shirt purchased went to the disaster fund. Soon they were selling like hot-cakes not only in Scotland, but all over the world.

Gray smiled. "I have some good news and some bad news on the shirts Hobbo."

Tony grinned. "Go on then."

"Well the good news is that they are selling as fast as they can put them on the shelves. The bad news is that I heard this morning that the Matembo number 10 shirt is out selling the Hobbes number 4 shirt by at least twenty times."

Tony shrugged his shoulders. "It's just yet another cross that we midfield cloggers have to bear. All anyone ever wants to know are the 'Fancy Dan' strikers."

Gray turned back to Simon. "Now then young man. I must ask you a little about your plans. I am sure that there must be a lot of clubs from all over the world chasing your signature. Any thoughts yet?"

Tony's face clouded and he was about to speak but Simon beat him to it. "I have not heard of any of this Mr Gray. My mother says that I must finish my school before all other things. I am very happy playing for Queens Park. They are a very great team. Do you know that they are the oldest football club in Scotland?"

Gray could not help but smile. "Yes Simon, I do."

The boy continued, very serious, very earnest. "It is a very good team for somebody like me. Did you know that they had the first black player to play in Britain?"

This caught Gray on the hop. He began to wonder who was actually interviewing who here. "No Simon. I never knew that."

"Yes Mr Gray. He was a man from British Guyana and he played over a hundred years ago. It is a very great honour to be able to play for a team with so much history. I am also lucky because they will allow me to play even though I am still at school and cannot become a professional for some time. There are not many teams like this I think."

"Well, there is one." Said Gray. "Scotland. They are obviously quite happy to have an amateur in the ranks, especially after the game in Rome. What are your thoughts about the England match in June?"

"Mr Gray. There were very many injuries before this game in Italy. Many experienced players will be fit by the time we will play this England game. I am only a young player. I do not think they can want me for this game."

At this both Tony and Andy Gray burst into laughter. Gray said. "Something tells me that Bill Duncan might just see things differently. Anyway, that's all for now. I would like to thank you both for your time here today and I must congratulate on you all your remarkable efforts for the appeal. Let me remind all of you out there that Sunday's game is available exclusively on *Sky Box office* for £8.00, all of which will go to the Relief Fund. To order the game all you have to do is . . ."

PAY FOR VIEW

A camera crew then filmed them as they travelled around. They visited the stadium that would hold the match on the following Sunday. They visited Rose at her college and took tea with President Kumba in his palace where he gave Simon a humorous ticking-off for adopting a British Passport. Finally they were flown by helicopter to Mapote where the chief took them on a tour of the damaged areas.

Tony was appalled at the devastation. The choking grey ash seemed to have coated everywhere and everything. However the prospect of the match had lifted everyone's spirits. Tony had arranged for the government to lay on buses so that the whole of Mapote could go to Kampala to watch their newly-adopted son. Despite the thick coat of ashes, it was still possible to see that building work on the new school was well under way.

The players arrived in Kampala on Saturday afternoon and they shared a hotel with the South African squad. Tony had a drink with their captain that evening and they agreed that the game should be competitive without being silly. Neither side wanted injuries.

The excitement in Kampala the next day was enormous. The small stadium couldn't begin to hold the many thousands who yearned to see the game. Karen, Ben and Tony's mum arrived on the plane on the morning of the match. They all told Tony that the interest in the UK was unbelievable. It seemed that the whole of Glasgow was wearing the green and blue shirts. Everyone wanted to see more of Simon. Andy Gray said that the number of advance bookings they had taken had staggered *Sky*.

It was well into the African night when the two teams took to the field. The crowd was a blaze of noise and colour. The mesmeric beat of hundreds of drums made the warm air seem to bounce. The pop groups had all performed and the stage was set. Presidents Kumba and Mandela were introduced to the two teams and at last the match kicked-off.

The South Africans were fast and skilful and they adapted to the hard, bumpy pitch much better. The Scotsmen soon realised that they were up against it and their professional pride made them play hard. The game was played at an unrelenting speed. At half-time South Africa lead by 2 – 1. The second half saw two moments of utter brilliance from Simon and the game eventually ended 3 – 3.

A jubilant Andy Gray came into the dressing-room soon after the final whistle where both sets of players were sharing a beer. He told them that *Sky* had sold in excess of two million "pay-for-view" packages. They had raised more than 16 million pounds for the relief fund.

Winston came over to Tony as all the players cheered at the news. He shook his son's hand. "Tony, I have never been so proud. No man has ever been so proud. You have done a very great thing here."

Another visitor came into the dressing room and the noise immediately died down. President Nelson Mandela was wearing the very widest of smiles. He came over to Tony and Winston.

"Now." He said. "You asked me for a favour and I was happy to help. Now it is my turn to ask for a favour. I know everybody must ask you the same thing but I demand to be placed at the head of the queue. I am visiting Europe next month and I would like you to get me a ticket for the game against England."

Tony grinned. "Oh, I think I might just be able to work something out."

Chapter 14
The Drums of Hampden

It took several days for everyone to get over the Ugandan trip but the whole of football was riding high on the staggering level of funds raised by the game in Kampala.

As April drifted into May and the season wound to a close, Scottish football was gripped by an excitement that it had never known before. The Simon Matembo story had become the biggest in the football world. Journalists from all over the planet flocked to Hampden for the next Queens Park home game against Brechin. It soon became clear that the demand to see the game was quite unbelievable. The club's stunned executives held a special meeting with the police and all parties agreed that for safety reasons the game would have to be made all ticket. The club management were collectively pinching themselves when every ticket was sold four days before the match.

The two teams kicked off to a carnival atmosphere. It seemed that almost the whole of the crowd was decked-out in the special shirts manufactured for the Kampala charity match. Not that all the hype had any effect whatsoever on John Craig, He stuck stubbornly to his plan and kept Simon on the bench until the second-half. The Matembo effect was by now having a dramatic impact on the other youngsters in the Queens Park side. Their confidence was running high and the noisy crowd carried them up to new levels of performance. By the time Simon made his entrance his team were already 3 – 0 ahead. Poor old Brechin didn't really know what was happening to them. The overwhelming noise of the 50,000 crowd was far too much. The match ended as an 8 – 0 triumph for the home team and Simon completed his second hat trick in Scottish football.

But of course the domestic season was a mere side-show to the main event. Tony and Simon had guided their respective teams to mid-table security in both of their leagues. For them the end of the season in May saw games which were more or less meaningless. The National Stadium was filled to capacity for both Queens Park's last two games. They finished the season fifth in Division Three. Partick avoided relegation comfortably and finished seventh in the SPL.

For many observers the most remarkable spectacle that Scottish football had seen for many years was the last Old Firm match of the season that was played out at Celtic Park in early May. The two Glasgow giants were locked together on level points at the top of the league and the match was clearly a vital one. As it turned out Rangers won a thrilling game 2 – 1 with a goal in the dying seconds. This was to be their springboard to claiming the title at the end of the month. Not that this was particularly remarkable in itself. The remarkable thing was that it seemed that almost every spectator in the stadium that day was wearing what had come to be known as a Kampala shirt. The passion of the 60,000 crowd was as intense as ever, but many said that the intense feeling of hate seemed to have disappeared.

At the end of the game both Tony and Simon joined the players of both teams who all changed into their Kampala shirts. They all did a lap of honour together to huge applause from every corner of the ground. At one point it seemed as if the stadium's roof would be lifted off as the crowd roared out "Flower of Scotland". Tony tapped on Simon's shoulder. He had to shout at the top of his voice in order to be heard above the tremendous noise.

"There you go Simon! This IS a song about a Scottish Chief. A very great Scottish Chief called William Wallace."

"Where does he live Mr Tony!"

"Tell you later."

In the week that followed there was much talk about the remarkable effect that the Kampala game had achieved. Had the simmering hatred of so many years finally been lifted? Some were doubtful, but many, many more felt that a dark time was at last drawing to a close.

Now that the domestic season was over the only thing that anyone cared about was the England game. Nothing else mattered. Nothing at all.

The nearer the big day came, the more the game was discussed. Journalists soon started to say that it was the most eagerly anticipated Home International that there had ever been. It did indeed have all the classic ingredients. England had stuttered badly, taking only one point from a possible six from their two home games. Even so, many experts believed that this was the finest English squad to be assembled for many years. Already the bookies had made them 3 to 1 second favourites to win Euro 2004 behind the mighty French. Scotland on the other hand had been little more than a hard working journeyman team before Simon made his remarkable impact in Rome. The 4 – 0 mauling that the Scots had received at the hands of their oldest of enemies at Old Trafford a few months earlier had left deep scars. Most experts agreed that without Matembo the odds would be stacked heavily against the underdogs.

To add to the excitement, the Italians, still smarting from their home defeat to Scotland, had gone out and murdered Luxembourg 9 – 0 in Turin. This meant that they had by far and away the best goal difference in the group. Things were on a knife-edge.

Team	P	W	L	D	Points
England	7	4	1	2	14
Scotland	7	4	1	2	14
Italy	7	4	2	1	13
Latvia	7	2	4	1	7
Luxemb'g	8	0	8	0	0

The maths of the group was relatively simple. England had a superior goal difference to Scotland, so a draw in their showdown at Hampden would be enough to take them through ahead of their British rivals. If Italy were to complete an expected victory over Latvia they would move two points clear of the Scots. In short, only one result was likely to be of any use to the home team – a win. Only a win would do.

England was certainly smarting. Only a few months previously they had been the darlings of the tabloid press. After the 2002 World Cup campaign, they had appointed a young Italian coach, Paulo Farelli, and the papers loved him. He was smooth-talking and always immaculately turned out in designer suits. As his team completed their pair of victories away to Italy and at home to the Scots he was hailed as a new Messiah. However things had started to turn a little sour. The papers were angry when England fell to a classic Italian counter-punch, and they were absolutely livid when they were held to a draw by a stubborn Latvian side To make matters worse, the Scots had become everyone's favourite team. All over the world football fans of all nations were united in their desire to see the fabulous young African and his Scottish team mates make it to the Euro 2004 finals. The huge amount of money raised for the Ugandan Disaster Fund had endeared the Scots to millions and millions.

This of course did not sit at all well with the English. So much seemed to have changed in the space of a few short months. They had gone from being a widely admired young side to the team that everyone wanted to see lose. They hated it and they withdrew from the media spotlight.

However sentiment only went so far. By and large the experts were unanimous that the English would have too much firepower for the Scots. They had talent and strength running right through their side, and in Jimmy Stamp they had a player of genuine world class.

Two individual battles intrigued everyone. First there was Tony against Jimmy Stamp. Stamp had been voted "Player of the Year" by both The Press and his fellow professionals. He had played quite magnificently for the whole season for his club, Manchester United, who had yet again won the English Premiership. He had become the hub of the England midfield. It was generally agreed that to stop England, you had to stop Stamp. Could Tony Hobbes do this? At 33, would he have the fitness and the stamina to hunt the Londoner down over the open spaces of Hampden? Most of the experts believed that he could not. He was too old. His day had passed.

Even more intriguing was the prospect of Simon Matembo being subjected to man to man marking by England's Charlie Mills. Mills had seen his career transformed since the arrival of the new Italian coach. For most of his career he had been little more than a run-of-the-mill hard-working midfielder for Aston Villa. He had never been the most skilful of players but he had always been regarded by his fellow pro's as being one of the fittest players in the game. He certainly had the reputation of being a ferocious tackler. Farelli gave him a new role. He turned Mills into a man to man marker in the mold of many of the great Italians who had done the job down the years. Mills was revealed in this new role in a friendly against Brazil when he had snuffed "World Footballer of the Year", Bedo, completely out of the game. At times his play was far from pretty to watch. But he was effective. Ruthlessly effective. He had collected eleven yellow cards through the season and he had become the man that all opposition fans loved to hate. There was little doubt who would be given the job of taking Simon Matembo out.

Bill Duncan was in constant demand for interviews. He was a man of few words at the best of times, and he preferred to say as little as he could get away with to the press. Tony received a phone call at home from the manager one evening.

"Tony. Bill Duncan here."

"Hi there Boss, you well?"

"Aye. Not bad. Sick of the sight of journalists though."

Tony groaned. "Tell me about it. I've had them camped outside the front gate for weeks now."

"I just wanted a wee word Tony. I've got a big press conference tomorrow. I think it might just be time to start playing a few little mind games with Mr Farelli."

Tony laughed. "You've been talking to Sir Alex haven't you."

"Aye, well maybe we might have bumped into each other at Ayr Races the other day."

"What have you got in mind . . ."

Once again the Media Centre at Hampden was packed. The questions rained down on Bill Duncan.

"Mr Duncan, Bob Hewitt. *Sky Sports*. John Craig has carried on with the tactic of using Simon Matembo for the second half only. Will you be doing the same?"

Duncan paused for a moment. "Look, I'm getting a little concerned with all this hype about Simon Matembo.

Remember, he only played in Rome because we had a chronic injury crisis. Everyone seems to be forgetting that he is just a boy. He's only seventeen and he's only played a handful of games in the Third Division. Now without being too insulting to our lower leagues, they hardly offer ideal preparation for a game like this."

"Are you saying that he might not even be in the squad!"

Duncan gave the journalist an angry look. "Of course I am. I have a full squad of players to choose from for this game. I can select experienced, battle-hardened pro's. This is not going to be a playground out there. This is Scotland against England. It will be hard, hard and then harder still. It's no place for boys out there . . ."

The Press Conference exploded into near chaos. The next day the back pages were plastered with the story. Before Duncan had said his bit it had seemed impossible that there could be any more hype surrounding the game. However the hype now went up to a whole new level. Would he play? Surely, he HAD to play? Could the Scots do it without him? Was Duncan playing games?

All the media hype soon got to Simon. Eventually he approached Tony. "Mr Tony, I know that school is the most important thing. My mother, she says the same thing. But I would like to play in this match. Just this one game. Even as a substitute."

Tony smiled at the boy. "Don't worry Simon. You'll be there. I am not at all sure that we can beat England without you. But listen, you must not say a word about it to anyone, not even Ben. We are going to keep them guessing. Every day that goes by will make them more nervous. They won't really know how to prepare. That is how we want it. OK?"

Simon smiled with relief. "Yes. This is OK."

"Now," said Tony. "In the mean time you are going to help me. Come into the lounge and sit down. We are going to watch lots of videos of Jimmy Stamp. He is good, really good, probably the best attacking midfielder that we have seen in ten years. He is clever with the ball and he is fast. He has a lot of tricks up his sleeve and he will use every one of them at Hampden. I want you to watch these tricks and learn them. There is nothing that he can do that you can't. When you have learned them we will go down to the training ground early in the mornings and you will try them out on me. OK?"

"Of course Mr Tony."

Throughout the last two weeks in May and the first week in June they went to the Partick training pitch a little after six in the morning. Time and time again Simon ran at Tony with the ball. To start with he flew by him two times out of three. By the second week Tony was able to make the tackle about half the time. By the end of the third week he got the ball three times out of four.

In the afternoons Tony cycled and swam. He went for mile after mile and length after length. By the week before the match he was fitter than he had ever been before.

During the last week Simon joined the team for training. They practised far away from the road so that nobody could watch. They worked hard on a variety of moves. Tony imitated Mills and he dogged Simon around the pitch.

Still Duncan said nothing about the team. When the players moved to their hotel by Loch Lomond on the Friday morning Simon went to school as usual. He drove up with the family later in the evening. They entered the hotel by the back door.

The next morning the nation watched the shots of the team getting onto the coach for the drive to Hampden. No Simon Matembo. There was almost a sense of misery in the television studio. Simon in fact had arrived at the ground with Winston before the coach had even left the hotel.

As kick off time approached the pundits in the radio and TV studios talked more and more about tactics. Andy Gray was sharing the *Sky* studio with Terry Butcher and Kenny Dalglish.

    GRAY: "So Terry. Tactics? What are we going to see out there?"

BUTCHER: "Well Scotland need to win. It's as simple as

that. The atmosphere is going to be beyond belief out there. I think that they will start very, very fast and hit the English with everything they've got."

GRAY: "So it'll be blood and thunder then?"

BUTCHER: "Course it will. This is England – Scotland. How can it be anything else?"

GRAY: "Kenny? What do you think? Do you agree with Terry?"

DALGLISH: "Course I agree with Terry. I always agree with Terry. Look at the size of him!"

GRAY: "But seriously, Kenny."

DALGLISH: "Well everyone seems to think we Scots are predictable. It's all Braveheart and blood and bagpipes. Who am I to argue?"

GRAY: "So you think Bill Duncan might just surprise us?"

DALGLISH: "Bill Duncan is a canny lad from Glasgow. Lots of folk have been surprised by canny lads from Glasgow."

GRAY: "Terry. Simon Matembo wasn't on the team bus. Do you think Scotland can do this without him?"

BUTCHER: "No. No I can't see it Andy. I know the atmosphere will be intimidating, but I just think that England have too much quality. Matembo would have given the Scots that little bit of something special. Without him? No. I can't see it. England 2 – 0. Hard game. But 2 – 0."

GRAY: "And how about Hobbo? Can he keep up with Jimmy Stamp?"

BUTCHER: "I like Hobbo. He's my kind of player. All heart. Three or four years ago I think he could have done it. Now? I don't think so. He's only just back from a heck of an injury and to be honest playing for Partick in the SPL is no preparation in a game like this. Stamp has been performing week in, week out for United in the

> Champion's League. He's too young. He's too quick, and to be honest, he's too good."

GRAY: "Kenny? Can Hobbo do it?"

DALGLISH: "Hobbo's an old Liverpool player. They teach you a thing or two down there. You should know Andy. We never gave you much when you were at Everton. Hobbo's still got it upstairs and that's what counts." Dalglish tapped the side of his forehead and gave a small smile.

GRAY: "Can they do it without Simon Matembo?"

DALGLISH: "Who says they'll have to?"

GRAY: "Bill Duncan for one. He's kept saying that it will be no place for boys out there."

DALGLISH: "Is that the same as saying Simon Matembo won't play?"

GRAY: "No, but he wasn't on the coach from the hotel Kenny."

DALGLISH: "So?"

GRAY: "So what are you saying, Kenny?"

DALGLISH: "I'm saying Bill Duncan is a canny lad frae Glasgow. I'm saying wait for the team sheet . . ."

That morning there was a new sound to be heard on all the routes into Glasgow. It was heard in service station car parks and on railway platforms. It was heard in the pubs around the city. It was heard in the streets that lead to the stadium. And as the time for kick-off approached it was heard louder and louder. It was the sound of drums.

An enterprising company had made the inspired move of importing thousands and thousands of small drums from a company in South Africa.

As the Scotland fans converged on Hampden it seemed that almost every one of them carried a drum. At first the stewards wondered whether they should be allowed into the stadium. They consulted with the policeman in charge. He decided that it would be against the new mood of the game to confiscate the drums. They were allowed in.

THE DRUMS OF HAMPDEN

As the players got ready in the dressing-room they began to hear the sound. It was an awesome sound. There were nearly 40,000 drums in the stadium and when they were beaten together it seemed to make the ground shake.

At their end of the ground the England fans were reduced to near silence every time the sound of the drums beat across the stadium. To go with the sound of the drums was the chant of "Matembo! Matembo! MATEMBO!" The England supporters had been convinced that Simon would not play. At 2.30 their hopes were shattered. The drums thumped hard when the tannoy announced Simon's name as one of the substitutes.

A record audience all over the world tuned in their television as the two sides made their way onto the pitch. Tony had been true to his word and Sir Robert had reserved a seat for Nelson Mandela next to his own in the Royal Box. As Tony lead his players out into a wall of sound he gave the President a wave. Mandela gave him a thumbs-up sign and waved back.

England had not dared to believe that Simon would not play and so Charlie Mills lined up alongside Jimmy Stamp in the centre of their midfield. At last the game was underway.

Scotland's tactics were simple. Instead of a blood and thunder approach they kept things tight and kept possession as much as possible. They had no intention of over committing themselves and allowing England to hit them on the break. It was a hot sunny day and the plan was to make England run around as much as they could. They weren't too concerned about creating chances. That could come later. That could come when Simon came on with half an hour to go.

In the first minute the ball flew out for a throw in and Tony jogged over to mark Stamp.

"Lovely afternoon Jimmy."

"Get lost Hobbo."

Tony laughed. "By the way Jimmy, I'm fit today. We'll see shall we?"

The opening exchanges were predictably tight and cagey. After ten minutes Scotland's passing was humming nicely. They patiently moved the ball around the pitch and made the England players chase and harry. The crowd soon cottoned on and every Scotland pass was met with a loud cheer.

In the 21st minute a pass went astray. England grabbed possession and fizzed the ball forward. In a flash Stamp was on the ball and sprinting for goal. Tony moved over to intercept. The Irishmen dipped his shoulder and made to move left. Simon had quickly mastered this trick. The secret was to flick the ball right at the last minute. Tony had faced the trick over 50 times in the last fortnight. He calmly stayed on his feet and waited for the move. When it came he moved easily into the tackle and claimed the ball cleanly whilst dumping Stamp to the floor. He stopped and pushed a simple ball out to the full back. He turned and pulled the shocked looking Londoner to his feet.

"Told you Jimmy. I'm fit today."

He read the Londoner perfectly a further three times in the first half and on each occasion he took the ball off him with ease. The confidence was beginning to drain out of Jimmy Stamp.

Simon came out of the dugout twice during the first half and jogged up and down the touchline. Both times the drums thumped into life.

"Matembo! Matembo! MATEMBO!!"

Tony sensed the nerves of the England players tighten a notch. They glanced over to Simon uneasily. Their self-belief was slowly ebbing away. Scotland was winning the mental battle.

The opening period of the second half brought more of the same. By the 50th minute England were starting to look tired. Their passes started to go astray and they were beginning to bicker with each other. Scotland continued to calmly roll the ball around the pitch.

A sense of anticipation started to spread around the crowd. In the 55th minute Simon once again started to warm up and this time the drums hit a new level of thunder. This time he would come on. Everyone knew it.

In the 60th minute the ball flew out for a Scotland throw in and Simon came on to deafening applause. The small tigerish figure of Charlie Mills trotted over to stand close by. To everyone's surprise Simon took up a position between the two central defenders. For ten minutes he never moved out of defence. He jogged easily around pushing short passes to and from the defence and the midfield. Mills followed him every step of the way and began to look slightly comical. On three occasions he attempted to scythe into Simon, but each time the African jumped out of the way with ease. In the 67th minute Tony gave him a small nod and he started trotting round in a circle behind the two centre halfs. An embarrassed Mills was forced to trot with him.

In the 69th minute Tony gave another small nod and Simon jogged back to his own corner flag and the Englishman duly followed whilst Scotland passed the ball around the midfield. When he reached the corner flag he simply sat down. A tide of laughter poured down from the Scotland fans that were massed behind the goal. For a moment Mills simply stood and stared at him. He then shook his head in annoyance and ran back to the half-way line. In the 70th minute Tony gave another signal. This time it was open and loud. He threw his right arm up and yelled. "GO SIMON! NOW!"

Simon spun away from Mills and sprinted down the right wing. The ball came to Tony who shaped to launch it towards him. The two England central defenders charged over to block Simon's run. Stamp launched himself into a desperate tackle to try and get the ball from Tony.

At the last second Tony dragged the ball back and Stamp slid past. Tony then twisted his body and clipped his pass into the huge empty space that had opened on the left of the England defence.

Bobby Simms had timed his run to perfection. He collected the ball with ease and moved into the box without a defender in sight. He walloped the ball into the right hand corner and the ground erupted.

The Scotland players mobbed Simms. They had

practised the move for hours the week before and it had worked to perfection.

England was destroyed. They had fallen for a sucker-punch that had been coming for a whole fortnight. They made half-hearted efforts to get forward but they were a beaten side. Simon once again fell back to the defence. Scotland caressed the ball around the pitch as their fans cheered every pass. England had given up chasing long before the ref at last blew for full time.

The next twenty minutes were a blur for Tony. He shook hands with a beaming Nelson Mandela. He joined in the lap of honour as the team saluted their jubilant drum beating fans.

When he at last made it to the tunnel he was breathless with excitement. A hand grasped his shoulder. It was Andy Gray. "Not so fast Hobbo. You still owe me remember. Over here. I want an interview."

"No problems Andy." Tony shouted over to where Simon was celebrating with two of the younger players. "Hey! Simon! Over here!"

Simon came over and Tony draped his arm over his shoulder as the cameramen got ready. As he looked beyond the camera he saw a small group had gathered in the tunnel to watch them. Winston and his mother stood arm in arm with Karen and Ben. The Chief and Thomas were both beaming with delight. Next to them Samuel was holding Rose's hand and smiling a shy smile.

It had been a long road and a strange year but it had ended in triumph. As Tony grinned at his family and friends his mind was filled with a single thought. "Could anything possibly ever be better than this?"

A sharp voice pulled him back to reality.

It was a sharp Scottish voice. "Hobbo! Wake-up will you! Right we're on. 3 – 2 – 1 . . . Tony, tell me, how long did it take you to develop those tactics . . ?"

Outside the drums of Hampden beat on late into the Glasgow night.

The End